THE FIRES OF HELL

Coming down the fjord, U-45 saw the debacle. The roar of the concussion, the sudden brilliant jet of flame, the wild swirling fling of debris, all told their own story.

'She's done for,' said Baldur Wolz. He felt sick. 'The Norwegians will pay for this,' said Forstner, savagely, evilly. He gripped onto the cold steel of the bridge and glared at the scene of destruction. 'They'll pay!'

The fuel oil spreading over the water caught fire.

Men trying to swim in that lake of fire screamed and thrashed. They could not breathe. The skin of their faces and hands burned and peeled and crisped. Horrors screamed and thrashed in the water. Dark heads showed among the flames of the burning oil. Hair frizzled and flashed. Eyes bubbled. Faces were stripped away to blackened skulls. . . .

SPECTACULAR SERIES

THE SGT. #1: DEATH TRAIN (600, $2.25)
by Gordon Davis
The first in a new World War II series featuring the action-crammed exploits of the Sergeant, C.J. Mahoney, the big, brawling career GI, the almost-perfect killing machine who, with a handful of *maquis,* steals an explosive laden train and heads for a fateful rendezvous in a tunnel of death.

**THE SGT. #2: HELL HARBOR—
THE BATTLE FOR CHERBOURG** (623, $2.25)
In the second of the new World War II series, tough son-of-a-gun Mahoney leaves a hospital bed to fulfill his assignment: he must break into an impregnable Nazi fortress and disarm the detonators that could blow Cherbourg Harbor—and himself—to doom.

THE SGT. #3: BLOODY BUSH (647, $2.25)
by Gordon Davis
In this third exciting episode, Sgt. C.J. Mahoney is put to his deadliest test when he's assigned to bail out the First Battalion in Normandy's savage Battle of the Hedgerows.

SHARK NORTH
BRUNO KRAUSS

ZEBRA BOOKS
KENSINGTON PUBLISHING CORP.

ZEBRA BOOKS

are published by

KENSINGTON PUBLISHING CORP.
475 Park Avenue South
New York, N.Y. 10016

Copyright © 1978 by Bruno Krauss
Published by arrangement with Sphere Books

All rights reserved. No part of this book may be reproduced in any form or by any means without the prior written consent of the Publisher, excepting brief quotes used in reviews.

Printed in the United States of America

CHAPTER ONE

Oberleutnant zur See Baldur Wolz gripped the cold metal mounting of the 8.8 centimetre and looked up at the conning tower as the harsh voice of Kapitänleutnant Forstner whispered down through the darkness.

'Remember, Herr Oberleutnant. Thirty minutes. Not one second more.'

What the fool would do if the rubber boat had not returned in thirty minutes, Wolz wouldn't like to guess. Probably shove off and leave him and the landing party as he threatened. This U-boat skipper was worse than a boil on the arse. But Baldur Wolz forced all emotion from his voice as he whispered back. 'Very good!'

Here they were, halfway up a Norwegian fjord with the cold cutting into them like flaying knives, a swirl of snow blinding down and thickening on every exposed surface, U-45 lying hove-to three hundred metres off shore in the darkness, and a landing party gone astray. Forstner had told Wolz very firmly that he was to 'bring that damned stupid bunch of idiots off at once' or the U-boat would sail without them.

How Kapitänleutnant Adolf Forstner would cope with his first officer and six men of his crew missing, Wolz was not inclined to enquire into; the idea made him laugh, and mirth was an emotion out of place here and now.

The stars glittered when the overcast shredded and the invisible scything veils of snow parted momentarily. The cold was the very devil. This was the beginning of the period of the new moon, the 7th to 15th April, 1940, and U-45 had been charged with the task of landing a mysterious passenger up Vesfnfjord. His task had not been revealed to the men of U-45; but it needed no genius to guess he was here in Norway to carry out important work for the Third Reich in the struggle against England. The British were going to invade Norway. They hated the thought that Swedish iron ore was being carried by the million tons to Germany, and they'd invade a neutral country and bring war against the iron ore fields, the railway and the ports to stop the traffic. Well, the Führer was well up to handling that kind of international piracy.

The water of the fjord was frigidly hostile, incredibly deep, and deadly. Wolz took great care hoisting himself off the steel casing and into the rubber boat. The rubber slicked cold and greasy under his gloved hands. He settled down and said to the nearest dark shadow: 'Give way, Fischer. And not a sound.' His own whisper barely carried.

The Norwegians were aggressively neutral. They'd shoot at whoever came prowling into their territorial waters. Once they'd been made to understand that the Germans came in friendship to protect them from the British, then it would all be all right.

Fischer laid his paddle gently into the gelid water and the other two men in the airboat took up the rhythm. Calmly, soundlessly, the rubber boat began to crawl across the pitchy water towards the shore. Thank God there was no wind to speak of. All the signs said there would be a blow coming up. Wolz just hoped U-45 would be safely out of this forsaken fjord and comfortably at sea by the time the muck blew in.

The darkness all about him betrayed no easily identifiable landmarks. But the coast showed as a dark blur. Inland, the mountains would lift up into the tangle of bad country. Often Wolz had felt thankful he had joined the Kriegsmarine, although he enjoyed a pleasant hike through the mountains of home, he knew damn well that if armies fought in this country there would be nothing pleasant about it. Maybe that was what this fellow U-45 had brought here was about. Maybe the Norwegians would accept the Germans as friends. Wolz sincerely hoped so.

The grating under the rubber told him they had arrived.

Getting out was a matter of importance, for although he, like all the men, was warmly muffled up, he did not much fancy squashing about in wet boots. They pulled the boat up a little and then stared about.

'Where they've got to is anybody's guess,' said Fischer. He was a loose-limbed, easy-going man from Stettin, who was renowned as having a good 2 centimetre flak gunner's eye. Now they stared about into the snow-filled darkness, feeling helpless.

'We'll find them,' said Wolz. Although he whispered he spoke incisively. 'Fan out up the beach. Keep walking in a straight line. Report back in ten minutes.'

So they began to spead out from the boat. Soon all Wolz could see through the splattering snow were the black bulks of the fjord-cliffs, rearing over him, swaying against the erratic glitter of the stars. The way down to the tiny beach lay ahead, the way he had chosen to go himself. Rocks grated underfoot. He checked, listening. The sounds of footfalls and the tumble of a rock over to his left made him frown. That would be Braun, a reckless devil, a torpedo man from Berlin who fancied himself a smart fellow. When they got back to U-45 Wolz would chew him out for making so much noise.

Another sound obtruded itself.

Wolz listened, trying to identify the source.

He had made up his mind that after the twenty minutes he had allowed he'd shout for Petty Officer

Lindner and the others. And damn the consequences. Something must have happened to them. Lindner was a sound man, a P.O. on whom to rely. And no one was running off in a place and on a night like this.

The sound came again, a gurgling kind of gasp, as though air was being forced through a blocked pipe.

Carefully, silently, Wolz stalked forward. The nine millimetre Walther P-38 in its new leather holster snuggled at his waist. He unsnapped the flap but did not draw the pistol.

The little snick of sound whispered and was lost in the night.

Snow settled on his shoulders. Flakes blew into his face, and he blinked. He could taste the cold wetness on his lips. A darker mass loomed ahead and he went forward even more cautiously. Here was where the little cove entrance led off the beach, with the rocks rising to either hand.

The sound came again, a gasping puff of effort, and then a voice, low, speaking German.

'It's no good, Hans. We'll never shift the poor fellow.'

Then Hans Lindner's voice.

'We've got to shift him, Kurt. Put some weight into it. And keep quiet!'

Wolz eased forward.

Was that the dim blur of men, moving, crouched? He peered through the swirling snow, and saw only blackness and half-glimpsed forms, with the hard ebon lift of the rocks beyond.

'Lindner.'

He spoke so as to break the inevitable shock.

Lindner reacted well.

A foot scraped on rock and the sound of a smack came, quite clearly. Then: 'Number One? That you, sir?'

'It's me. What's gone adrift?'

Wolz moved in. Lindner's bulky figure was vaguely

their bodies warm in those spots the struggle with the rock had left cold.

'It's got to go,' snarled Wolz. 'Again!'

The strain tore at his arms, and drove his head back in a gasping rictus of pure effort. All the world was a single scarlet pall of effort. He could not feel his fingers at all.

The rock moved a fraction.

They collapsed, gasping, coughing.

'One more time and we'll have it,' said Wolz. He looked down on the unconscious man. Whoever he was, if they saved his life he would owe them. If he was Gestapo – well, Wolz knew Cousin Helmut was Gestapo, now. All the old suspicions had crystallised. But there was no time to be dreaming about shore leave and home, the schloss of Uncle Siegfried that was home to Baldur Wolz. Now they had to rescue a fellow-German.

'Shift your grip along a trifle, Schmundt. Get close to him, Lindner. That's better.' With the other two on the far side, and Wolz heaving from the end, this time he felt they would do it. If they didn't then they wouldn't.

'This time,' he said. The snow drove down in a gust and the sound of the wind freshened, to die away.

He took a good firm grip, not feeling the rock, only knowing his hands were two claws under the splinter, gripping, holding, ready to lift. He took a breath –

'Now!'

The rock shifted. It grated. For perhaps five centimetres it rose.

Fischer hauled frantically.

With a lurching smash of utter finality the rock dropped back into position. A rock chip flaked away and spat into Wolz's leg. The rock trembled.

But Fischer drew back, standing up, a dark shadow in the star-lit snowflakes.

'He's clear.'

'Then hoist him up and let's get back to the boats.'

'What about Schmidt, sir?'

'Yes, bring him along. We can't leave a dead German seaman cluttering up a neutral beach, can we? The locals wouldn't like that.'

So, with an unconscious man and a dead man between them, they trudged back through the darkness and the falling snow to the rubber boats. Lindner's boat had beached fifty metres off from Wolz's. They split the passengers and crew and paddled out. Wolz took a single flashlight glimpse of his watch.

They had been away twenty-nine-and-a-half minutes.

Grimly, he turned the torch seawards. He flashed out U-45 twice, and stowed the torch away and seized a paddle. If that idiot Forstner followed the book – or his own stupid orders – and left them here, they'd be hard put to it to survive. They'd have to find shelter, at the least. Probably the Norwegians would find them, and then it would be internment.

Baldur Wolz did not want to be interned.

He was no fire-eating S.S. officer, no fanatical Party man; but he believed Germany was fighting a just war, a war into which they had been forced by the intransigence of the decadent democracies, and as Germany was going to win the war and it would be all over soon, he did not wish to be deprived of his share. Duty, to Baldur Wolz, was a concept he had heard a lot about, and ignored, and come to terms with in his own way. He understood Germany's position in the world and was glad and proud that the Fatherland was once again a power to be reckoned with. The Führer had brought the country back from ruin, had given her people dignity once more. Baldur Wolz was not prepared to allow his country to be ruined again.

Paddling with powerful but silent strokes, the U-boatmen urged their rubber boats out across the three hundred metre stretch of water separating them from U-45.

When the darkness ahead coalesced, turning lumpy with the vaguely visible outlines of a U-boat sitting motionless in the water, Wolz owned he felt a thump of distinct relief.

Had Forstner taken U-45 out as he had threatened and left them stranded, internment would have been only a part of what they would have had to face. This damned cold! It tore at a fellow's guts. Wolz's hands were mere ice blocks now and his feet had gone past the aching stage. He wondered as the two rubber boats splashed alongside the U-boat's steel casing if his feet would fall off when he took off his boots.

This was a damned different kettle of fish from that last cruise in U-42!

The men climbed out and hauled up the unconscious agent and the dead body of Schmidt and then hoisted the rubber boats ready for deflation.

They moved with the practised perfection of well-trained U-boat men. And there was need for hurry. Already the darkness was giving way to a pallid silver light. Up here in these high latitudes at this time of the year the day and night cycle was shot to hell. U-45 must be away before early light.

Seeing that the deflation and stowage of the boats was well under way, and Schmidt and the agent passed below, Wolz climbed the ladder to the bridge.

The slight form of Kapitänleutnant Adolf Forstner on the bridge seemed to Wolz to represent all the things he heartily disliked about this brave new Germany.

'So you are back, Herr Oberleutnant?'

Wolz quelled the desire to make an offensive reply.

'Yes.'

'Well, get below. We must dive at once.'

'Very good.'

Wolz put his booted feet on the steel ladder and lowered himself down thankfully. Forstner had seen the two bodies. He would demand explanations the moment they had dived. The clang of the closing hatch told him that moment had arrived.

The Engineer Officer, Leutnant z.S. Loeffler, busied about the business of taking U-45 below, had time only for a raised eyebrow. Wolz nodded; but said nothing. The skipper must have the details first, despite he was an offensive obscene member in the crew. Water from the cold Norwegian fjord gushed into the tanks. Pumping engines began to whine. The air intake shut off and the diesels died. The electric motors took up the task of turning the twin screws, filling the boat with that almost indefinable thrilling vibration. U-45 slid beneath the water, a steel shark for the moment baffled of prey.

Kapitänleutnant Adolf Forstner dropped down the ladder through the kiosk into the control room. In the harsh white lighting, his face with its fringe of dark beard and the two brilliantly blue eyes looked gaunt, almost adolescent, frighteningly young for a man in command of a U-boat and responsible for the lives of forty-four fellow men – forty-three now that poor Schmidt was dead.

Forstner stood blockily on his heels, his head tilted back, for he was a short man. He regarded Wolz balefully.

'Well, Herr Leutnant? And what mess did you make of it back there?'

'There was a rock fall. It killed Schmidt and trapped our passenger. He was unconscious and probably wounded.' Then, out of malicious spite, Wolz added: 'Probably the rock fall was occasioned by the cold.'

Forstner gave him a look.

'So you brought him back?'

Wolz's face did not move a muscle. Finally, he moved his frozen lips enough to say: 'Yes.'

'This is a fine mess. B.d.U. were most insistent. We had to deliver the fellow at the right place and the right time. We're here and now he goes and ruins it all.'

Forstner bit his lip. 'What kind of consideration is that?'

Wolz did not feel called upon to answer.

The boat shuddered – only a little, only a fraction, and Wolz put it down to that fractious starboard motor that had given Chief Engineer Loeffler trouble ever since they'd left Kiel – but the Kapitänleutnant swung away from his First Lieutenant, his thin bearded face ugly.

'Herr Leutnant Loeffler! If you cannot maintain trim and service in this boat I shall have to put in a report on you!'

'Very good,' said Loeffler, half-turning, going aft in a hurry. He'd work some miracle on the motor, enough to make it deliver a few more thousand revolutions before it played up again. Wolz saw Loeffler's face. That broad, good-natured face with the hint of ginger in the hair and incipient beard, that broad squashed nose, that firm, full-lipped mouth, indicated quite clearly what Loeffler thought of the skipper. But discipline held them all, the iron discipline of the Kriegsmarine, and, more, the steel discipline of the U-boat arm. Loeffler hurried aft without another word.

Forstner said something half under his breath, which Wolz ignored.

How the fellow had got himself into U-boats was something Wolz did not begin to understand. He was a dedicated Party man; but that meant nothing when Admiral Dönitz selected officers to command U-boats. The Party had made scant inroads in the Navy, a fact for which Wolz had at one time felt sorrow and now could feel only thankfulness. He had never himself been free of the Navy from an early age, and he had never joined the Party, although urged to do so by his cousins. Ever since his father had gone down in his U-boat at the end of the last war, stupidly rammed by a German minesweeper, only a few days before Wolz had been born, the fates had decreed that the son should follow in his father's footsteps. That had not seemed at all probable when Wolz had been a child; but the Navy had built U-boats in secret, for Spain and Finland and then, with the Führer and the promise of a great Germany once more, the chance for the U-boat arm of the Kriegsmarine had come again.

Baldur Wolz was a child of Nazi Germany. He had devoted his life to the enthusiastic following of the destiny that seemed to him marked him as an ace U-boat commander. Well, he had started in fine fashion and he meant to go on in the same way. All the Party idiots like Forstner were not going to stop him.

And, anyway, there were excellent U-boat commanders who were Party Members. The current Number One, Gunther Prien, surely, for his fantastic effort in sinking the British battleship *Royal Oak*, was a dedicated Nazi. Prien might be a rough egg, a tough and competent man who knew exactly what he was doing; he was still a fine U-boat skipper. Wolz, his fair hair catching the boat's lighting and gleaming golden, wondered where Forstner had gone wrong.

'Herr Leutnant,' said Kapitänleutnant Forstner, regarding Wolz with that distant look of veiled dislike. 'It seems you have made a hash of it. As soon as our passenger is recovered and we can lie off here again, you will take him ashore. And, this time, Wolz, see that the job is done correctly.'

CHAPTER TWO

With the familiar sound of a submerged U-boat about him, Baldur Wolz ducked through the bulkhead door into the wardroom. Leutnant z.S. Ehrenberger, the Second Officer, had the watch. Wolz removed his soaked outer clothing; but in these latitudes, in a U-boat, clothing became wet and stayed wet for the rest of the patrol. This was a perennial discomfort which U-boat men accepted with a grumble and accustomed themselves to as best they might.

A cup of coffee, at least, could warm him a little. The coffee was good, certainly, even if he would have preferred English tea or the scalding hot kai of the Royal Navy. The Blacksweat of sailing days conditioned a man's stomach to accept all kinds of foul drinks. Wolz sat on the leather settee across one end of the wardroom and pondered.

This Kapitänleutnant Forstner was a pain. The debacle on the beach had been none of his First Officer's doing. The facts were that Wolz had retrieved a tricky situation. But Forstner seemed to think that blood and iron meant the absence of brainpower and of simple human consideration. Wolz had met his kind before, and had turned away, not caring to waste time on them.

Here, as the First Lieutenant of U-45, he could not turn away from his skipper.

The hum of the electric motors evened out. The Chief came back into the control room and reported all well.

Forstner merely grunted an acknowledgement.

Then Wolz heard him snap out in his hoarse penetrating voice: 'Take her up to periscope depth, Herr Leutnant.'

'Very good. Periscope depth.'

The Chief could manage the evolution, which could in certain circumstances be extremely tricky, with an effective display of skill that always impressed Baldur Wolz. The compressed air hissed into the tanks, driving out the water. The boat came alive, rising through the water levels.

The hands were well-trained, that was also sure.

U-45 had been through a fraught experience last October in which she had been sunk and most of her crew killed. She had been salvaged and raised and recommissioned and Kapitänleutnant Adolf Forstner placed in command. Wolz had heard talk that U-31, sunk by a Bristol Blenheim in the Schillig Roads on the 11th March, was also to be salvaged and recommissioned. U-31 had taken with her many good men, and Wolz, like all U-boat men, was grimly aware that many more good men would die in U-boats before the end of the struggle.

As for himself, since his rescue by U-40 after he had been abandoned in his Bachstelze by U-42, Wolz retained the firm conviction that he was living on borrowed time, that by rights he should be dead, and therefore he might do anything at all with impunity, for he had already been past the point of death. The future opened up to him filled with giant possibilities, a new age, and one in which he meant to make everything he could from every last second, for every last second could in truth be his last.

The boat moved smoothly through the water. Wolz felt the swaying rhythms of underwater movement soothing him. The Third Officer, Leutnant z.S. Meyer, favoured Wolz with a puzzled, almost apprehensive look. Wolz took no notice. Meyer was cowed by the commander. Well, they all were, of course; but in Meyer's case oppression must have taken an evil turn. Wolz, who had welcomed his appointment as First Leutnant to U-45 with great joy, now wished that the original First Leutnant had not stupidly got himself killed. Wolz would have fared better out of this boat.

There were things to be attended to. The corpse of Schmidt must be properly buried. The unconscious agent, a limp bulk flung on to a bunk and left to the mercies of the sanitatsobermaat, had to be revived. He might not, as Forstner had so blithely assumed, agree to be dropped in the same place a day late.

The thought occurred to Wolz that this one day's delay in carefully calculated plans might throw everything out. Perhaps as a result of that rockfall on a Norwegian beach the Germans would be too late to protect the Norwegians from the British. Perhaps the course of the whole war could be affected.

He stood up, a little stiffly, and went across to the bunk.

The agent lay flat on his back, his head half-turned, looking decidedly unhealthy.

The sick berth attendant worked on the cut and bruises on his head. He looked up as the Number One appeared.

'Anything serious, Reche?'

Sanitatsobermaat Reche shook his head.

'Difficult to tell. There are these cuts and bruises on his head – well, the falling rock did that. But his insides...'

'No bones broken?'

'No. I'm sure of that.'

'Well, he'll come around soon enough, I don't doubt. Do what you can for him, Reche. We want him off the boat. We can't start our patrol until we've dumped him ashore.'

'Very good!'

At periscope depth, U-45 cruised gently through the water. Forstner's face betrayed nothing beyond his habitual ill-temper as he checked the depth gauges, and nodded.

'You seem to have brought us to fourteen metres well enough, Chief. I congratulate you.'

Wolz moved into the control room in time to hear this, and to see Loeffler's reaction. The Chief's mouth twitched. A muscle jumped alongside the corner of his mouth, twitching up his cheek. But he merely nodded his head and said: 'Thank you, Herr Kapitänleutnant.'

Wolz felt pleased.

Pick the bones out of that one, you bastard, he thought pleasantly to himself.

One up for Loeffler.

Forstner gripped the ladder leading up the conning tower.

He climbed up and settled down on the saddle seat.

'Up periscope!'

The tube slid up with an oily hiss. Wolz cocked his head up. Only the commander could see what was going on in the big outside world. Wolz had overcome any early feeling of being trapped. They were trapped, in reality, trapped in a steel tube beneath the water. But he had forced himself to face that and rationalise it out. The commander saw what was going on and gave his orders and the boat's crew carried those orders out instantly and perfectly, otherwise...

One day, one day, Baldur Wolz said to himself, one day he would be a U-boat commander and the whole machine would function at the behest of his brain and will.

'Steer three-four-five.'

'Steer three-four-five,' repeated the helmsman.

The tube was still up.

Wolz fretted. Forstner had the periscope sticking out of the water for a damn long time.

They were out of the fjord now and in the awkward way of things the deep water of the fjords shoaled rapidly just offshore before the deeper water could be reached. U-45 must cruise offshore until the night and then take the agent ashore again. But Wolz, like any U-boat man, would seek every opportunity to charge his precious batteries. He cursed Forstner out of the pit of frustration that held him trapped as much as he was trapped in the steel pressure hull of the U-boat beneath the sea.

The Second Officer, Ehrenberger, glanced at Wolz and lifted his eyebrows. Wolz kept his face frozen. The periscope was still up.

What the devil was the fool playing at?

But, then, anything could be going on up there, and only the commander could know. Clearly, the horizon must be empty. If the English were invading Norway today, and any of their aircraft or surface units were in sight, then Forstner, at the least, must spot them.

Baldur Wolz sincerely hoped so. It was his neck, too...

At last, at thankfully last, Forstner rapped out his orders.

'Down periscope. Take her up, Chief.'

'Blow all tanks! Surface!'

With a smothering billow of white water and a surge of foam, U-45 broke the surface. Forstner led the way up, clanging up the steel ladder, throwing back the hatch. Wolz followed him through the hatch on to the bridge and instantly was staring intently all around the compass.

Nothing.

Only the shore of Norway, away to the east, and a smooth but uneasy sea all about them, green and grey and endlessly moving. Slight overcast hazed the light. It would be a day of reasonable weather, cold, bright with that penetrating and yet muffling irradiation of brilliance of these northern latitudes. A day of charging batteries, then. Of charging batteries in more than one sense.

Baldur Wolz took his duties as First Lieutenant of U-45 very seriously indeed. Whilst he was always the first in the fun and games that made life endurable, he would tolerate no slackness, no inefficiency, no slightest falling-off from the very high standards required of the U-boat arm. He counted himself fortunate that in the U-boat arm the keenness of the men, their training and discipline and morale, were all of the highest. He regarded himself as being entrusted with the care of the men and having to continue to maintain already achieved perfections. If he could improve on perfection, he would, for that was his way.

But – and it was a vastly ominous but – this wart Adolf Forstner presented problems that interfered with the way Wolz considered the boat should be run.

He could always make a private report. That would endear him to no one, really, for problems must be ironed out at this level. He hungered for the command of a boat, for his own boat. He had already tasted what command was like, in U-42 when Kapitänleutnant Gustav Ludecke had been incapacitated, and the taste remained sweet. But – always a damned but!

But he must deal with Forstner, maintain U-45 in perfect trim – the pun did not escape him – and so contrive it that no blot appeared on his record.

The task appeared daunting.

One small, yet tremendously revealing, fact emphasising the enormity of the problem lay in the way of the crew of U-45 never called the commander Daddy, in the usual affectionate way of U-boatmen. The men in U-45 might call their commander skipper; but that was as close to familiarity as they would go.

The breeze was beginning to disperse the overcast. The light brightened deceptively. Objects which were a long way off could appear as close to; and you could stare for seconds at something right under your nose and mistake it for some object miles away. A day for caution.

The sea washed away each side over the bulging saddle tanks, creaming and swirling, so that the water coiled at a man's mind. The steel saddle tanks looked like two sea monsters eternally following the ship. Wolz looked hard at each man of the watch, making sure each had his glasses in use, and each covered the quadrant for which he was responsible.

Forstner, after that first look round and the drawing of deep breaths of that cold air, went below. His white cap vanished through the hatch. Wolz, in turn, took a breath. Now, for a space at least, he was free of the incubus.

But that, too, was illusory, for the wart would find fault no matter what happened.

This day would pass like any other day. Tonight they would drop the agent, if he had recovered sufficiently, and then they could begin their offensive patrol. If any English warships came up here attempting to land troops, or escorting troopships, then U-45 would bag a few. A steel shark of the sea, the U-boat would fulfil her destiny in life by dealing death.

When Lottie's mother had died, there had been some terrible scenes, for Lottie, for all she was a romp and a moist sweet lovey, remained still very much a child. Wolz thought of the way she'd cried, and his clumsy attempts to comfort her, the chill earth of the grave, the mist over the cemetery, the moisture-laden, drooping trees, the blackness of it all – God, what a series of thoughts to cheer a fellow on U-boat patrol in freezing weather off Norway!

He should, rather, be thinking of what had happened the night of the funeral. His Uncle Siegfried had done all that was required of a close friend. His aunt had been visibly upset. So the youngsters, and there were fewer of them now that the war had continued long after any reasonable man would have considered it over, had taken themselves off to Cousin Manfred's room to console themselves and to sympathise with Lottie, who was staying overnight in the schloss.

Manfred's room was masculine, filled with trophies of sports and flying, a pair of skis braced against one wall, a splintered propeller on another, relic of his first solo. A swastika banner hung over the door. Photographs of aeroplanes adorned the walls. Pride of place, of course, had been given to Willi Messerschmitt's Bf 109. The best photo of that remarkable single-seat fighter showed Manfred leaning from the cockpit, smiling, confident, at ease. But all the other photos and technical drawings were of English aeroplanes. Wolz knew them all, as he must, Spitfire, Hurricane, Hampden, Wellington, Whitley, Sunderland – at the Sunderland he looked with the ruminating pondering of a man studying a personal antagonist.

'All ready to be shot down, Baldur!' explained Manfred, fishing out the schnapps. They were on to spirits by this time. 'Know your enemy.'

'The Sunderland,' said Baldur, eyeing Lottie's friend, Heidi, who draped herself on the arm of a chair so that her skirt slid up. Damned minx. She knew what she was doing, too well.

'You've nothing to fear from that fat cow,' said Manfred, grandly. 'The Sunderland lumbers along like a pig in farrow.'

'Oh, we'll have our moments, I don't doubt.'

An army Hauptmann of the Panzers, his pink waffenarbe very fancy, hauled his girl into the embrace of the sofa with one hand and balanced his schnapps with the other. He'd done well in Poland, so Wolz had heard, and Manfred had struck up an acquaintance with him in Berlin on some staff duty. There were three young men and three girls, and Manfred's eyes were fixed on Lottie, who, all sauce and impudence gone after the funeral, clearly wished to find some comfort and sympathy from Wolz.

Wolz gave his cousin a look. Manfred, sturdy and outgoing and fair-haired, a scatterbrain fighter pilot of the Luftwaffe, stared back, puzzled.

He winked.

'Heidi's aching for it, Baldur. Why don't you – ?'

His sideways glance indicated the bedroom beyond. Heidi tossed her head. She was nice. No doubt of that. Wolz had found her to be grateful, also, after he had discovered her being assaulted against her wishes by a drunken Hauptsturmführer of the S.S. under the backstairs. But he was in the mood to turn his back on offered sweetness and seek to share the pain suffered by Lottie. He might be a fool, he might even be a masochist – although he doubted that, doubted that with a cynical laugh, by God – but the thought of Lottie, poor, silly Lottie, affected him.

He said to Manfred, low, head bent: 'You deal with Heidi tonight, cousin. I don't think Lottie is in the mood.'

The Luftwaffe officer glanced up. His brows drew down.

'I see what you mean, Baldur. But – Lottie needs – '

'She needs peace and quiet and, perhaps, a shoulder to cry on. I do not think she needs what you can give Heidi.'

So Manfred took himself off with Heidi. The Panzer Hauptmann was crawling all over his girl, spilling liquor on to her dress, making her squeal. Wolz looked across at Lottie. He knew her well enough, knew her face, knew her body, knew her artless ways. He forced the thoughts of two other women from his brain. He hadn't seen Trudi since his return from patrol; and had found no excuse to visit the neighbouring castle and he had run full tilt into an unexpected mental resistance to going deliberately. His days with Trudi lay ahead of him. He was determined on that. As for his Cousin Lisl . . . as always, he could not think coherently about her.

Lottie stood up. Her face shone red and lumpy in the electric wall lights. She looked at the photograph of the Sunderland, her head cocked to one side, some pins loose in her hair, her long evening gown caught about one leg.

'So this is your enemy, Baldur.'

'One of them.'

'It looks – clean.'

Wolz laughed. 'It's a big lumbering old cow and we'll be safely down at forty metres long before it's anywhere near.'

'And then you'll be safe?'

He picked up his drink and twirled the stem, a deliberately theatrical gesture; but one which his sense of drama testified was apt. 'Safe enough. We can go down another sixty if we have to. The depth charges won't reach us there.'

She looked across him at the Panzer officer and his girl. They were passionately entwined on the sofa, and long silk-clad legs thrust into the air. A pink-edged jacket with brave silver insignia flew up, caught on a silk-clad toe, slid, fell to the floor, knocking over a glass. Drink spilled.

Lottie did not smile.

'I feel such a cheat,' she said. She swallowed. Wolz saw how brilliant her eyes were. 'You men go off to war, and I stay here and create such a fuss – '

'We have only one mother to lose. I was lucky.'

'Lucky? You mean, because you were too young to understand?'

'No. I don't think it matters how young you are. You know. Even if you don't know you know. Lottie – '

'So how were you lucky?'

'Because I was young. Not too young to understand, but young enough to miss the pain. Or, if I felt pain and didn't know I felt it, then not old enough for the pain to mean anything to remember – that I can remember.'

'I think I see – '

She bent down, very gracefully, and lifted the hem of her long gown. The material shimmered in a shifting coloured pattern of greens and reds and blues as the light caught it. She reached up with a few expert pulls and drew down her silk camiknickers. They were pink. She balled them and threw them across the room at Wolz.

'Catch!'

'Lottie...!'

'Manfred and Heidi are in the bedroom and these two here are where we ought to be. Standing. I think I would like that.'

'But – ' He did not know how he felt.

He walked across to Lottie and put his hands on her shoulders. She turned her head. He could feel the thump in him, the same old thump. The camiknickers under his fingers felt soft and warm, warm with the heat of her body, musky, exciting. He might think he knew Lottie; but she remained always fresh, a remarkable romp, remarkable...

'Baldur, my mother – she's gone, and, and – '

He bent and kissed her.

When their lips parted, she said: 'I know what I want, Baldur. I don't think you do.'

'In one thing, I do.'

'Oh, yes, to command a U-boat. But I mean know about the important things in life.'

'What is more important than commanding a U-boat!'

'Here, you foolish boy...'

She took his right hand from her shoulder and forced it down. He felt her waist, the swell of her hip, her thigh. Her fingers trembled against him. He lifted the long dress.

'Now, Baldur. Now, hard and brutal and don't give a damn! Just do it!'

For some reason, Baldur Wolz did not think he would enjoy the experience. It was not his style. But, as they stood up together, he felt excruciatingly that this did, indeed, bring a new dimension. He could not forget the girl – he did not think he could ever do that – but her demands stemmed from the needs in her. By negating her as an individual as she demanded, he exalted her in one special way. He was barely conscious of all that. He was aware only of her body pressed close to him, of her breath on his cheek, of the way she responded.

Yes, a fine romp, Lottie.

When he let her go and drew back and her shimmering dress fell demurely back, he said: 'And next time we do it –'

'Maybe there won't be a next time. I think I shall become religious.'

'That won't go over well, not these days.'

'Perhaps not.'

She was primping her hair, and licking her lips. Much of her pallor had gone. Dots of colour spotted her cheekbones.

'You'll be all right, Lottie? Your father –'

'He is worried because the army have cancelled some orders. Now there doesn't seem the same urgency to buy guns and tanks.'

Wolz, in his morose mood, refused to say what lay uppermost in his mind. He kissed Lottie again, saying: 'You were right, Lottie. But, next time, and there will be a next time, we'll use the bed. It's more civilised.'

She laughed. It was the first time she had laughed since her mother died.

'Civilised? You, Baldur Wolz, civilised! Why, darling, you're the most savage barbarian I know!'

That crushing remark remained with Baldur Wolz.

He still didn't know if she meant it in raillery, as a mere matter of general information for his benefit, or if, sharply and horrifically, she meant it because he was a U-boat man and sank ships and killed and drowned their passengers.

CHAPTER THREE

Through the hazy mist that clung uncomfortably about ears and eyes and mouths, and with a thin feeling of cold cutting through the marrow, the men of U-45 took their boat back again into the fjord.

Oberleutnant z.S. Baldur Wolz stared through the mizzle, trying to make out what, if anything, lay across the dark waters. The agent had recovered, complained of a damned headache, eaten enormously, and had then declared himself fit and ready to be landed again tonight.

'Sooner him than me,' observed Leutnant z.S. Ehrenberger, and laughed, a little ruefully, as Wolz had pushed past to go into the conning tower.

It would snow again, that was for sure. The cold inside the pressure hull was always intensified, of course, as was the heat of the tropics. That was the humidity in the boat. That and the higher pressure from the inevitable leaks from air-pressure lines made life uncomfortable at best and downright devilish at worst.

Wolz stared carefully about. There had been reports of British submarines. A large number of British submarines prowling off Norway – well, and what did they want here if there was to be no invasion by their forces? The Swedish iron-ore traffic was carried in neutral waters, along the Leads, and was inaccessible to them.

Befehlshaber der Unterseeboote had given strict orders, and when B.d.U. ordered, U-boat commanders jumped. Admiral Dönitz was a man who knew his own mind, knew what was best for the U-boat arm and fought for them accordingly.

A vague blur of deeper darkness through the mizzle showed Wolz the cliffs of Norway. He flipped the lid of the voicepipe and gave a low-voiced order. The U-boat angled her course, her diesels muffled, easing along at eight knots, going cautiously. There was plenty of water beneath them here. No sense in taking chances. The mouth of the fjord was about to open up and Wolz would take her through dead centre. Kapitänleutnant Forstner had left precise instructions to be called once they had entered the fjord. The agent would be ready. Then it would be up to Baldur Wolz to ferry him ashore. After that, perhaps, they might get back to the business of being an operational U-boat.

The blur receded. The water held that grey greasy look, barely visible, that told of all the unpleasant things a shipwrecked man would not wish to dwell on. The depth readings came up the pipe and Wolz nodded thoughtfully, his mind ticking off the readings as he related them to the chart he held in his brain.

Then the hydrophone operator broke in, speaking quickly, yet his voice in perfect control.

'H.E. bearing one-six-five. Slow revolutions.' A fractional pause, and then: 'Diesels.'

Wolz said: 'Can you hear – ?' and stopped speaking abruptly as the hydrophone operator went on, rapidly.

'Propeller effect changing. I can't quite . . . That's odd . . . Sounds like a lavatory – '

If the hydrophone operator didn't know what he was listening to, Wolz most certainly did.

'Dive!' he yelled and hit the button.

'Down you go!' he rapped at the lookouts, and grabbed the inevitable slow one by the collar and fairly threw him down the hatch. One-and-one-fifth seconds per man. If they were down in fifty seconds, that would be reasonable, twenty seconds if they were quick. He felt his body tensing up, awaiting the impact, and forced himself to drop down the hatch, feeling the motion of the boat about him, seeing the water roar surging up the deck towards the conning tower. Water slashed at him, then he was down and could reach up and drag the heavy hatch shut. It clanged like the last trump. He span the wheel, clipping up, breathing hard, and for a moment he hung there, almost but not quite panting, as though he had run a fast hundred metres.

At the command 'Flood!' the ballast tanks had been opened and sea water had rushed into the steel tanks, driving the air out in spuming spouts from the upper valves.

Wolz dropped through the tower.

'Get forrard!' he yelled.

The hands knew what was wanted. They rushed through the narrow, instrument-encumbered tunnel of the pressure hull, cramming themselves as far forward as they could, huddling up against the butts of the torpedo tubes.

The extra weight forward would drive U-45's bows down that much faster.

Wolz glared around the control room. Only the personnel on duty remained.

Kapitänleutnant Forstner exploded through into the control room from the wardroom. He looked mad clean through.

'What's going on, Wolz? I gave no orders to dive now! We've a job to do!'

Wolz ignored him for the moment, his eyes on the depth gauges. Loeffler had the boat under control. He'd trim out at forty metres and the men could come rushing back to take up their proper positions. To move about the boat without orders was a crime.

'Herr Leutnant Wolz! What is the meaning?'

'Listen,' said Wolz, and cocked his head up.

Everyone heard the roar overhead, like bacon slicers

going at full revs, a tearing rush through the water.

'A British submarine loosed torpedoes at us. The eels would have ripped us apart if we'd loitered about up there.'

'Well,' said Forstner, and then he quietened down. He looked distinctly green about the face. He swallowed.

Then he recovered himself.

'If we didn't have this important passenger to disembark,' he said, with a fine show of bravado, 'there's nothing I'd like better than to stalk the bastard.'

'Yes,' said Wolz. He made himself say that and no more.

'He missed,' said Loeffler, with some satisfaction. 'Forty metres.'

'Resume stations,' said Wolz.

The men came back, pushing past, knowing what was to be done. They were a good bunch, well-trained. Wolz could have made a top-class U-boat from this crew, and given them a record second to none. But he was second to Forstner, and was not allowed to forget it.

'We won't surface just yet,' said the commander. He looked about. 'Slow ahead on the starboard motor only – '

'It would be best to use the port motor,' said Wolz, stiffly. 'The starboard is playing up.'

Loeffler nodded.

'I gave my orders,' said Forstner. His face held a pinched, almost petulant look. 'But as you are so concerned over the Chief Engineer's function, Herr Leutnant, we will use the port motor. And keep her at a good trim, d'you hear?'

'Very good!'

What could you do with a fellow like this? Wolz didn't know. The situation appalled and disgusted him. There was no chance to talk man to man, even as second-in-command to the skipper. It was all heel-clicking and by the book – if only the First Officer of U-45 hadn't had his fool accident! Wolz would have been in the Baltic working up in a new boat and almost any skipper in the U-boat arm would be better than this cretin.

They'd had a near escape. The Englishman had lurked in ambush, right in the best position. He'd been parallel to the coast, facing the fjord, and anything going up presented a nice fat broadside target,

Almost of its own volition, Wolz's mind began to calculate out the necessary evolutions to stalk the English submarine, to steer the various courses to bring him into a good angle for a shot. And then he realised that Forstner had kept them submerged. They had entered the fjord, just. Now was no time to be creeping along beneath the water. The water was deep, well and good, but a fjord was a place to take your bearings with exactitude before you dived.

Ehrenberger looked across at Wolz. Well, that would do no good. Meyer, the Third Officer, looked away. He was completely under Forstner's thumb, was scared of the man, and could be left out of this kind of manoeuvre.

Loeffler had caught a good trim and U-45 proceeded gently through the water.

Wolz took a breath.

'The Englishman is well astern by now.' No further reports of H.E. had come through from the hydrophone operator. 'I'd like to take a look around aloft – '

At once he realised he had phrased it wrongly.

Forstner put his hands on his hips. He looked up at Wolz, although Wolz was not a tall man. His face held that thin-lipped sneering look of disdain that passed as strength of character among his kind. Wolz never passed a judgement on another man until he was forced to do. He had no wish to condemn Forstner, even now. But he was sombrely aware that the time of judgement came nearer with every fresh encounter with this wart.

'So *you'd* like to take a look aloft, Herr Leutnant. *You'd* like to run this boat, is that it? I am in command here, and it will go ill with you if you forget that.'

'I do not forget that, Herr Kapitänleutnant.'

Forstner's nostrils pinched in. He realised they must go to periscope depth and see what was going on. Everyone was aware of the tension within the boat as well as they were aware of the jagged cliffs to either side. The fjord narrowed sharply here before opening out. There was only one thing the commander could do.

Had he waited, wondered Wolz, would Forstner have realised that himself, given the necessary orders, taken them up without this gratuitous prod? Somehow, Wolz doubted it. More and more he was finding his disgust at Forstner's actions as a man and a commander turning into sheer fright at the man's attitude.

Had some surreptitious pressure been applied to get him command of a boat? That seemed impossible, given what Wolz knew of the U-boat service. But from what he knew of the Party, it might not be so wild a surmise as he thought.

The U-boat arm was dangerous, there was no doubt of that. But it held enormous attractions, and a certain type of man would be drawn with fascinated compulsion towards the ideas of U-boat service.

As Forstner gave his orders and U-45 lifted through the water, Wolz wondered with a shiver of shock if he was that kind of man. Was that what Lottie had meant? Was he a savage barbarian? Did the idea of torpedoing a helpless ship fill him with glee, satiate some deep blood-lust? Could he be that kind of butcher?

Gradually, the various restrictions imposed by Hitler on the conduct of Dönitz's U-boats had been removed as the war progressed, so that now a policy more in keeping with unrestricted U-boat warfare was in operation. That, it seemed to anyone who looked at all carefully at the position, was the way to smash England. Did this mean that Wolz was merely a sea pirate, sinking and burning without compunction?

Well, of course, he would sink and burn without the kind of compunction that meant nothing. He did not enjoy seeing fine ships sinking, of seeing and hearing men die. But these were mere parts of the whole. This was modern-day warfare carried to a logical conclusion. By these means the war would be ended more quickly, and thus in the long run many more lives would be saved.

The attitude of compunction was susceptible to many interpretations.

He remembered saying to Lottie, as she stepped into her camiknickers and hoisted them up her stockinged legs, the suspender belt straps very alluring, that he couldn't see any difference between doing what Manfred's colleagues in the Luftwaffe did, what the Wehrmacht did, and what he did. They killed civilians in the course of their operations. What was the difference between dropping bombs on Warsaw and torpedoing a ship?

Lottie had given a final tug and straightened up, and had shrugged those delectable shoulders, and suggested they find another drink. For, she had added, with a smile, his idea of a bed next time ought to be followed up very quickly.

The muttering rumble of the MAN diesels reverberated from the confining cliffs. U-45 crept carefully across the gelid waters towards the beach. Now was the moment when the waiting Norwegians would spring their trap, if they had been alerted by last night's fiasco.

In moments, perhaps, the cliffs would echo to gunfire and shells would come blasting in to rip and shred the boat, to spill the screaming crew into the icy waters. Wolz scanned the shore through the night glasses. He could make out only shadows, the hint of the beach exit, a swirl of night mist. Nothing appeared to move.

'Well, Herr Leutnant. What are you waiting for? Someone to hold your hand?'

'Clear away the boat,' snapped Wolz to the waiting crewmen. He held his temper down. Discipline was born and bred in the German spirit. This, he could cope with.

The rubber boat hissed and swelled. It took shape. Fischer and Lindner handed down the paddles to Schmundt. The passenger came on deck. He was well-muffled up and carried his bag tucked under his arm, secured by a strap. He was handed down into the boat and sat in the sternsheets, crouched, looking more frail and miserable than ever. Wolz did not envy him his job, whatever it might be. He felt pretty confident he'd never see the man again.

With a last check to make sure everything was ship-shape, Wolz stepped down into the boat. The lines cast off. The paddles dug in. They were on their way to the beach.

This time Wolz waited at the waterline for a few moments. The darkness pressed in. The cold cut cruelly. But he waited.

Then: 'Right. Off you go. And – good luck.'

The Walther 9 millimetre in Wolz's fist was a poor weapon if the Norwegians opened up with machine guns. But everything remained quiet. The stones under foot rattled. The beach exit looked dim and ghostly, like the entrance to some gelid hell.

'Thank you, Herr Leutnant. I hope we shall meet again.'

Wolz repressed his surprise.

'And I, too. Go carefully.'

The agent vanished into the shadows.

The three crewmen returned to the rubber boat. Wolz stepped in, the paddles dug, the boat span and turned and settled on course for U-45.

The job was done.

So easy, so damned easy. But for that fall of rock all this would have been done the preceding night, and U-45 could be away from this ironbound coast, out hunting British ships.

The familiar noises of water bubbling into saddle tanks, of air escaping with a hiss, of the surge and rush of water over the steel tanks and hull, reached the men in the airboat.

Wolz peered ahead.

He whipped out his torch and flashed. U-45. U-45.

No reply came.

The noises dwindled in a final rush of bubbling water.

The men paddled frantically.

They span in the boat as disturbed water caught at their fragile craft. The rubber boat span in the turbulence. U-45 was nowhere in sight. Wolz could scarcely believe it.

'The damned idiot! He's dived. He's gone off and left us!'

CHAPTER FOUR

The cold bit. The men huddled, shivering.

Wolz would not return to the beach.

There was no reason he could see for Kapitänleutnant Adolf Forstner to have dived U-45. But the fool had done so. The men abandoned in the rubber boat would have to wait for the boat to surface.

The wait would be a freezing hell.

'The commander must have seen something,' said Hans Lindner. As a long-service Petty Officer he could be a little more free. But, like them all, he was bound up in the steel regulations of the Kriegsmarine.

'Did any of you hear anything? See anything?'

Wolz looked at the dark bulky shapes in the boat with him.

'No, sir. Nothing. Not a thing.'

'Well, *something* must have happened.'

P.O. Lindner scuffled around under his heavy clothing. He held out his hand to Wolz.

'Here. Some chocolate. Special stuff, from Belgium. Not much of it left now, they tell me, back home.'

Wolz felt pleasure.

'Thank you, P. O. That is kind of you.'

Then Hans Lindner half-laughed.

'We're all in the same boat now.'

'If the boat does not surface within two hours of what they call daylight around here, we will return to the beach. Then we'll see about finding shelter. But, for now, we must assume the commander will return for us.'

One of the men, in so low a growl Wolz could not tell which one, said: 'If the idiot ever does.'

Wolz let that pass.

Discipline could be enforced in various ways. Wolz was developing his own ways. And upbraiding a crewman who shared his own point of view in a small rubber boat in a Norwegian fjord with the cold everywhere tearing at them, abandoned to their destiny, was no place and time to create trouble. The men – and he would have to reprimand all three – would feel sullen. The guilty one would feel guilt, the others would feel resentment. And all three would know he did not mean what he said. The stupid attitude of Forstner was too well known.

Wolz reflected that his clear duty on return to Kiel or wherever they were sent, would be to report Forstner as unfit for duty. That would be a highly unpopular move. And if there was any truth in his suspicions that Forstner had wangled his appointment, then the powers supporting him would have no mercy on a mere Leutnant-zur-See who thwarted their plans for their protégé.

But that last consideration should have no weight; the U-boat was too precious to have one of its units entrusted to a man like Forstner.

Dönitz must have approved him. The deviltry must have taken place at the Periscope School at Kiel. There they must have slipped up – that seemed the only explanation.

No doubt a stickler for Prussian discipline would have damned and blasted the men in the rubber boat there and then. That would have been one way. But Wolz felt he had learned a little. He was pretty confident that he had no fear of what might happen if he disciplined the men now. They'd take it. They were trained to take their medicine. But the incident seemed to him either too petty or too grave for immediate consideration.

And if he was making a mistake, then the hell with it.

He thought he was doing the right thing.

He hoped he was doing the right thing.

He fancied he knew what he was doing.

Lindner let out a little sigh, a susurration of the air before his lips. He pointed.

A periscope plopped into view about five metres abaft the boat.

It rotated.

A dark bulk below the water spread beneath them.

'She's coming up right under us!' said Wolz. 'Paddle clear!'

The water swirled all about them.

White wavelets splashed and rippled away.

They paddled frantically; but they did not move.

In horror Wolz felt the rubber boat tip and topple.

They were caught on the barrel of the 8.8 centimetre gun. The rubber boat swung wildly. Fischer fell out, yelling. Schmundt caught the line looped around the boat. Lindner had a grip on the gun barrel. And Wolz was sliding helplessly down from the boat, flopping out, sprawling on to the deck where water sloshed and splayed as the U-boat rose to the surface.

In seconds he'd be over the side and into the drink. The water would paralyse him.

If he didn't get a grip on some secure purchase he was a dead man.

'Herr Leutnant!' yelled Lindner.

Fischer, screaming, fell all asprawl into the water. He splayed his arms and legs, like a beetle, churning foam. He went under. Sluggishly, he rose to the surface and a wash of disturbed water caught him, threw him up, sucked him back towards the ballast tank.

Wolz fell to the water-spouting deck and rolled. He

felt the water bite at him. The deck struck him a hard blow and he gasped. His flailing hands felt the steel, felt the hard angular edges of the venting slits over the casing. Desperately he hooked his fingers into the slots. He held on.

His body dangled over the side. His feet kicked at the bulging metal saddle tank. He flailed around, trying to hoist himself up. The metal cut into his fingers. He was being dragged back into the sea by the weight of his body, the tug of his water-sodden clothing. He gasped with the effort of holding on. He could just hear a man screaming.

A bulky mass crashed into his legs. He twitched his head down.

Fischer sprawled across the saddle tank, gasping, his face a pale blur. Water bubbled about them.

Wolz let go with his left hand. He reached down. He tried to get a grip on Fischer's collar. The effort of unbending his clawed fingers and then of forcing them to fasten on the man's collar exhausted him. He felt the thick water-sodden cloth under the leather jacket. He felt his fingers slip on the greasy leather where water slicked. He made a grab and he could not make his fingers hook, could not get a grip.

Horrified he watched Fischer, his face upturned, his arms outstretched, his eyes pleading. Fischer slid slowly back off the saddle tank. He fell into the water. Wolz, dangling from one arm with scarlet pains shooting through his whole body, and yet numbed, numbed all the time with the pains zig-zagging through him, saw Fischer slip into the water.

The man slid into the water feet first and slid on and down.

He did not come up again.

Then hands gripped Wolz under the armpits. He was hauled up. He was brought inboard and hoisted like a side of pork, hustled along the deck and up into the conning tower, passed from hand to hand, passed down the hatch. The familiar odours of a U-boat assailed him; the mingled stench of oil and pitch and stale cabbage and human odours. He was aware of the kiosk going past his body, he could not feel the hands easing him through the lower hatch. He tried to stand up in the control room and the brilliance of the lighting blinded him.

He saw Forstner, a blur with a halo about its head, and he lurched forward.

Strong hands held him back. His body burned like ice.

'Forstner, you murdering fool!' he shouted.

'Silence, Herr Leutnant! You do not know what you are saying!'

Hands gripped his elbows, his arms. He was drawn back. Somehow he was in the wardroom and they were taking off his leather packet. He was wet through. They laid him out and someone pressed a cup of hot coffee to his lips. He drank, tasting nothing, feeling the nausea in him. He fell back, closing his eyes.

What had happened? How had the idiot brought the boat up directly beneath them? If Forstner had eased her up, gentled her up, he could have beached the rubber boat comfortably on U-45's deck. But he'd come bursting up like those Yankee cavalry galloping to the rescue. He'd tipped them over. The 8.8 centimetre had done for them. He'd thrown them into the drink. And Fischer was dead because of it.

Baldur Wolz's head flopped back, slipped to the side. He could feel nothing. The wardroom, the whole world, span away in a whorl of coloured fire. And the colour of the fire was the colour of ice.

Kapitänleutnant Adolf Forstner came through into the wardroom. His thin, petulant face was set in an expression of active dislike for his First Lieutenant.

Wolz sat with his back shoved against the sofa, his

body shaking, feeling the pains in him like the scarlet shooting branches of a tree tunnelling into flesh and blood – he was recovering; but he'd been damned-well almost off his head.

The sight of Fischer slipping down the saddle tank, his arms outstretched imploringly, his eyes wide and filled with horror – no. No, Wolz wouldn't forget that in a hurry.

'He's a little better now,' said the sanitatsobermaat.

Wolz accepted the cup of soup and drank. The stuff tasted like soaked cotton wool, flavoured with machine oil. He shivered.

'Get out,' said Forstner to Reche and the sanitatsobermaat scuttled out. The commander and his Number One had the wardroom to themselves.

In a low voice, leaning forward, staring at Wolz, Forstner said: 'I shall overlook what you said, Wolz. I shall not forget it. But we have a patrol to run and I need loyalty from my men. However, once we are back in Kiel I shall take the necessary steps.'

'Court martial?'

'You need not sneer, Wolz. Are you a German officer or not? If you knew what I know – but that is beyond you. No. No, I do not think a court martial will be necessary.'

A hidden amusement surfaced momentarily in Forstner. Wolz lowered the soup. He wondered what Forstner meant.

'We have been ordered to proceed to a rendezvous off Oslo. B.d.U. gave precise instructions. Ehrenberger has laid off the course. We must arrive early on the 9th.'

'No reasons given?'

'What do you think? Of course not. We shall receive further instructions then. But I warn you, Wolz. Although I have overlooked this matter at this time, any future misconduct will be treated by me with harshness. I am not satisfied with the conduct of the crew of

U-45. I command this boat. Should you ever forget that again, it will go hard for you.'

Wolz considered that Forstner was emphasising too much. That, he fancied, came from the man's feelings of weakness. He must know that he had been promoted into his position and appointed to a command when better men had been passed over. If Forstner really tried anything nasty, Wolz made up his mind to think very carefully about going to see Dönitz. It would make him unpopular. But if he had to, he had to. The good of the U-boat arm must come first.

For all his good intentions, he could not stop himself from saying: 'I gather you enjoyed yourself at Periscope School.'

Forstner's face pinched in.

'I do not know what you are talking about.' He stood up. The maze of piping and wiring beyond him gave him the look of a savage beast tamed in a cage. 'I have friends, yes, that is true. And I warn you, Wolz, my friends will not be pleased with you. You are running yourself into destruction.'

Caution at last caught up with Wolz.

He said, coughing as he spoke, feeling sick: 'I have only the desire to be a good first officer and to carry out my duties correctly. I will say, however, that had U-45 been brought up with some thought to the safety of the men in the rubber boat –'

'That is enough! I will not hear another word.'

Forstner turned towards his cabin, hidden beyond the green curtain.

'You had better make sure the boat is functioning perfectly, Herr Leutnant. I shall not tolerate any more mistakes.'

'Very good!' snapped Wolz, and choked back bile.

The night of 8th to 9th April, 1940, pressed down in darkness all about them, with a hazy mist. The moonless sky lowered above and the sea heaved with an uneasy motion. U-45 slid through the water, a long grey steel shark of potent destruction. Moving slowly and with caution the U-boat purred on her diesels up Oslofjord. Just before midnight she was well up inside the mouth. Her lookouts strained their eyes through the darkness.

Kapitänleutnant Forstner and Oberleutnant Wolz stood on the bridge, the Zeiss handy. The lookouts were on their toes. U-45 burbled through the water, going north, going north to Oslo.

'I can't see a thing,' complained Forstner. He wiped the Zeiss, roughly, as though blaming them for the absence of the moon, and the mist and the darkness.

Before Wolz could answer a flash split the darkness astern.

Moments later the report of a shot rolled up the fjord.

'We may not be able to see the Norwegians,' said Wolz quite calmly, although he did not enjoy this situation. 'But it is evident they can see us.'

The main force steaming up the fjord, darkened, ready, would be much more likely to attract attention than the low silhouette of a U-boat. All the same, Wolz felt annoyance that they had failed to see the patrol boat. For that was clearly what it was.

'Keep your proper lookout!' snarled Wolz as the lookouts automatically turned to stare aft.

He trained his glasses over the boat's stern.

More flashes, the sounds of gunfire, the rapid staccato of machine-gun fire – then a burst of flame and the rippling rolling sounds of explosions. A ship had blown up. Wolz just hoped she was not a German vessel.

'We ought to – ' began Forstner. He was jittery. His narrow body twitched in the conning tower.

'The orders from B.d.U. were explicit, I understand,' said Wolz. He derived no satisfaction from this. Their job was to precede the main force and report, to scout for them, to sniff out problems. Whatever had happened back there had happened. The briefest flicker of a light snapped at them through the misty darkness.

'All in order. Proceed.'

'Thank God for that!'

U-45 prowled through the water towards the small Norwegian forts on their tiny islands of Rauøy and Bolaerne. No sign of life was visible and darkness held them thralled. But Wolz tensed. They must have been alerted by the patrol boat in the mouth of the fjord. The gunners must be standing ready.

The main force had left Kiel at three o'clock on the 8th and, consisting of the panzer-schiff *Lutzow* and the heavy cruiser *Blucher*, with the gunnery training ship *Brummer*, and other units for special duties, was a balanced force of great power. Oslo had to be secured before the British invaded Norway. That was plain. B.d.U. had given exact instructions. Wolz, pondering what he would do if he were in Rear-Admiral Kummetz's shoes, formed a tactical plan in his mind.

The smaller forts ought to be disregarded and the force steam on through. The trouble might come if –

Forstner, swallowing loudly, put his head close to Wolz's. He spoke in a low tone, uneasy, fretful.

'Should we signal back all clear? There is no sign of life over there, although this haze makes it all so difficult.'

'The main force can steam through here safely enough.'

Wolz kept his tones incisive, devoid of the contempt he felt for this man. He rammed the Zeiss against his face and did not look at the commander. 'Further up, at the Drøbak narrows, is where we must look out.'

He felt absolute confidence that *Lutzow*, with her good armour and her six 28 centimetre guns, could steam past, followed by *Blucher* and the others. A few rounds ought to smother the batteries, even though they contained three 28 centimetres on the island of South Kaholmen. These were old guns, dating from 1892. They would be good guns, for they had been built by Krupp.

On the island of North Kaholmen there were torpedo tubes; but Wolz understood the German plan to trust in the speed of advance, audacity, and courage to burst through. Anyway, why should the Norwegians shoot? They needed the friendship and protection the Germans were bringing.

Strict orders had been given that the Germans were not to fire first.

If the Norwegians were misguided enough to open fire, then, of course, the Germans must reply.

Evidently, from the fireworks back there, someone had pulled the trigger. But the night was dark again, and silent, the mist hung over the dark waters, and U-45 eased along untroubled. Once past the Oskarsborg Fortress complex, Oslo would welcome the German fleet.

'But the minefields . . . ' Forstner's voice strangled in his throat.

'I doubt if they are even in place, let alone ready to be operated. They are controlled. Surely the Norwegians know we come as friends and to protect them? Why should they try to blow us out of the water?'

'You understand nothing, Wolz! How can you be so damned naïve?'

Forstner's words bewildered Wolz. And, as he had noted before, Forstner used bad language, a thing not generally liked in the Kriegsmarine. But – knowing nothing? Naïve? There were secrets in this new Germany of the Nazis, that was certain, and he did not pretend to understand a great deal of what went on. Being away in the Navy had a great deal to do with that. But he would not be goaded.

'You do not feel called upon to explain?' he said as the U-boat glided on in the misty darkness.

'Why should I waste time with you? You do as I tell you. I am an important man, Wolz, and don't forget it. I am as well aware as you of the Drøbak Narrows problem.'

That, inevitably, made Wolz let a half-smile crack the harsh line of his lips. He rolled the unlighted black cigar between his teeth, near grinning, relishing the pompous foolishness of this man as an entertainment, and hating it as an example of the man's danger to all in U-45.

'Yes,' said Baldur Wolz. 'The Drøbak Narrows Problem.'

Gliding near-silently through the night, with the slurred wash of water over the saddle tanks, the casing a mere dark shadow before him as he leaned from the bridge, the stars hidden in the shifting haze, the echo of gunfire in his mind, how could he take this idiot Forstner seriously? A treacherous desire to burst into laughter seized him.

He fought that down.

He had never known his father, that ace and expert submariner who had so criminally been sent to the bottom in the tangled wreckage of his U-boat by a fellow-countryman's minesweeper; but Wolz felt somehow very close to that dead U-boat man this night.

The soundings came up regularly; plenty of water to dive if necessary. That, as always, was a comfort. The tension increased as U-45 crept up the fjord. The shadowed masses to either hand assumed a greater solidity. Wolz kept the Zeiss to his eyes, studying the shoreline intently through the night glasses.

To their starboard on the mainland there were searchlights and 15.0 centimetre and 5.7 centimetre guns. The dark mass remained obscure; anything could be going on there.

To port, the island of South Kaholmen, black and ominous, showed a few dim lights, which flickered momentarily and went out.

Thoughtfully, Wolz considered the position. He had now persuaded himself that Forstner was unable to cope with this situation. If Wolz wanted to decide matters he would have to act with exquisite tact. Maybe he couldn't do it. Maybe the contempt in him would flare and strike violent sparks from Forstner. But he must make the attempt.

'The fireworks back there must have alerted the garrison,' he said. 'The Norwegians will be able to spot the big ships even if they cannot see us.'

'That will make no difference, Herr Oberleutnant. At the slightest sign of resistance, we shall open fire. After that, these Norwegians will know who is master here.'

Wolz quelled his impatient reply.

'In my view, Kapitänleutnant, the batteries are manned and ready to open fire unless some signal is made to them. If they expect us in friendship, why should they fire?'

'I do not wish to reprimand you again, Wolz! We go through, come what may.'

'Yes, I agree that. But –'

'Are you arguing with me, your superior officer?'

'No.'

'Very well, then. We go on.'

Wolz took his cigar out and rolled it in his fingers. He did not chuck it overboard; but stuck it back into his mouth, gripping with his teeth. The unlighted cheroot stuck up arrogantly from the corner of his lips. Blast the idiot! The situation seemed plain enough. Why was Forstner creating all this mystery? What was there in his orders he had not confided to Wolz?

Now U-45 wound her way between the narrowest point. A slight course correction, taking them angling to starboard, put South Kaholmen and its three 28 centimetre guns on the port quarter.

Wolz pivoted and looked back, down the fjord.

At that moment a searchlight was unmasked on the starboard shoreline.

It shone with a hazed and brilliant finger of light, stabbing the darkness.

The light played for an instant on the upperworks of a ship. Wolz saw. With camera-like immediacy he saw the ship, the powerful upperworks, the single funnel, and the two forward turrets. Two turrets, one superposed on the other, each carrying two guns.

'That's not *Lutzow*!' he said, astounded.

'*Blucher*,' said Forstner. The light went out and darkness fell back. 'Really, Wolz, you should brush up on your ship recognition.'

Wolz gripped the cigar so tightly it was almost bitten through.

'We must signal the flagship,' he said. 'At once. Tell–'

'Tell them what? That a panicky first lieutenant of a U-boat is scared? That he sees bogey men all around in the darkness? Really, Wolz, your conduct is scarcely becoming that of an officer of the Kriegsmarine.'

Again Wolz had to bite down all notion of a reply.

He stared aft. Acutely, he felt disaster threatening. He could not explain that weird feeling. It was eerie, it was uncomfortable, it was downright offensive. But, nonetheless, he felt the fey on him strongly.

If he was in command he would have to consider which of three alternatives to take. He could order an immediate one-eighty degree turn and retrace the course down the fjord. That would be running away. He could order the ships to open fire on the forts; that would be a blatant act of war. Or he could signal the forts, try to clear up the misunderstanding. The last alternative would be the one to choose...

Admiral Kummetz chose not one of Wolz's alternatives.

He chose a fourth.

Serenely, with darkened ships, at twelve knots, he steamed on up the fjord in neutral waters, carrying on as though nothing had happened.

Wolz looked at his watch.

It was 0515.

A few minutes later the guns fired.

The Oskarsborg fortress bared her teeth.

Wolz saw the livid flashes, saw the belch of flame as the 28 centimetre shells struck *Blucher*.

'No!' he cried, standing there helplessly on the bridge of the U-boat, watching a proud, heavy crusier of the German Navy taking a hammering.

Blucher's superstructure, clearly visible in the fires swiftly and devastatingly raging on her decks, showed a mass of twisted metal. It looked as though the gunnery control position had been shot away, and as Wolz stared the blast of a shell blew the bridge down on to the fore gun turret.

He stared, appalled.

Probably the soldiers in the ship had stored ammunition on deck. Petrol as well, probably. That had ignited. Flaming, she struggled on. She was still basically intact, her engines and boilers undamaged, for she surged on, spewing flames. She could still steam. She'd make it past the fort, clear the guns, get through. Then the fires could be got under control...

'We must go back,' snapped Wolz. 'We must go to her assistance!'

'Silence, Herr Oberleutnant! Our orders call for us to go on – we do not turn back.'

Wolz gripped the rail and stared with fury upon the proud ship surging up the channel. The guns fell silent for a space and then opened up on *Lutzow* and *Brummer*. *Emden* was back there, too. The flak from the ships fired, long spitting tracers curving through the air; but

Blucher's main armament remained silent.

The ship spouted flame and smoke. Wolz fancied she tried to increase speed; but she had been sorely wounded. He could see in the lurid light jagged holes rent in her metal. The noise of the guns boomed and crashed over the water. The smoke luridly illuminated by the flames, belched away, coiling, and was driven into fantastic shapes made all the more intense by the concentrated conflagration.

She was past the battery. She was still moving, still struggling on, crippled but still moving. *Blucher* came abreast of North Kaholmen.

Wolz saw and heard the two massive explosions against her side.

Two torpedoes from the shore installations ripped into her.

She tottered on for a hundred metres or so. Then with her engines out of action, she anchored in deep water.

'I don't believe it,' Forstner was saying, over and over. 'I don't believe it.'

Wolz looked at the commander. The light was brightening now. The flames from the doomed ship flared and flickered and grew and drove the daylight back; but the night was passing.

Some houses on the shore had been set alight by *Blucher*'s flak. The ship hung on her anchor, burning. How long she would take, Wolz did not know; but he could guess at the frantic efforts on board to fight the fires. He judged the fires to be almost past the controllable stage.

'We will have to go back and render assistance,' he said, and started to give the order to the quartermaster in the kiosk.

Forstner bellowed: 'Belay that order! Herr Oberleutnant, we have our orders. We are to go on.'

Wolz pointed at the flaming wreck of a once proud cruiser.

'There are men in her! She's done for. We may have our orders; but orders are one thing. Duty is another.'

CHAPTER FIVE

Baldur Wolz could taste salt bitter and slick on his lips. He chewed down savagely on his cigar, glaring at Kapitänleutnant Forstner, his words hanging between them like a challenge.

The commander's face betrayed all the malevolent fury of a weak man knowing his weakness and unable to reach a decision, faced with a colleague for whom he harbours only contempt and yet in whom he sees powers of decision he can only envy and hate.

Wolz did not work these thoughts through coherently. All he knew was that there were German sailors back there facing a fire that would at any moment burst past all control. There would be many deaths.

'Our orders are explicit, Herr Oberleutnant.' When Forstner added the 'Ober' to the 'Leutnant' he was up to something, instead of his usual arrogant self. 'I am an officer of the Kriegsmarine and I do not disobey orders.'

Wolz took his cigar out of his mouth, slowly. He said: 'The English talk about "The Nelson Touch". Do you know what that means, Herr Kapitänleutnant?'

'I care only for the English that I should sink them. We go on up the fjord in compliance with our orders.'

The wan northern daylight showed snow and bleakness and stark hillsides, with the burning houses adding a macabre note of death amidst the scene. The flames from the burning cruiser lay along the water like flung bloodlines, traceries of fire, reaching arms of death reflecting in the holocaust.

Men were jumping from *Blucher* and struggling ashore.

Lutzow pumped a few rounds at the Oskarsborg Fortress; but she could do nothing against the emplacements, ancient though they were.

Wolz turned back to his commander.

'We must go back to render assistance.' He saw the manic light flare into Forstner's eyes, and he went on ruthlessly. 'We are to scout ahead of the main force. Well, where is the main force? Nothing is passing the Drøbak Narrows until those batteries are silenced.' He gave the cigar a twirl, and said, very nastily: 'As the commander of the U-boat detailed to scout this force, you would do well to think what your higher authorities will say about this disaster. At the least, you may retrieve something by being seen to act with energy and decision in rescue work.'

Wolz had kept his voice low and penetrating so that the lookouts could not overhear.

In the same half-hissing manner, Forstner started to sneer back a bitter comment. But then the meaning of Wolz's words penetrated.

'Yes – ' he said. And stopped, and fingered the growth of beard fringing his chin. 'Yes. There is always that.'

Perhaps, Wolz considered, and thinking the thought ridiculous even as he entertained it, perhaps this fool didn't realise how disastrously he had carried out his orders, or, rather, how his actions would be viewed by the admirals who ordered life for the Kriegsmarine.

'*Blucher*,' said Forstner. The word was almost a groan.

'It seems to me *Blucher* is gone. If the flames reach a magazine...'

'They will flood!'

'If they can.'

'Those batteries, how could we tell they would open fire?'

Wolz did not feel called upon to make a reply. Clamping his black cigar into the corner of his mouth he flipped the lid of the voice-pipe and gave the quartermaster the reciprocal course to steer. He looked up at Forstner. The commander's maxillary muscles jumped; but he did not speak.

U-45 turned one hundred and eighty degrees, carefully, and began the return down the fjord.

Pouring smoke and shooting flames high into the air, the German heavy cruiser took on a greater and greater list. She was heeling over to near twenty degrees. Many men had already reached some kind of safety; but others remained in the ship to fight the fires.

Coming down the fjord U-45 saw the debacle. When a magazine for the 10.5 centimetre guns exploded, the fate of the ship was sealed. The flooding valves had been out of reach. The roar of the concussion, the sudden brilliant jet of flame, the wild swirling fling of debris, all told their own story.

'She's done for,' said Baldur Wolz. He felt sick.

'The Norwegians will pay for this,' said Forstner, savagely, evilly. He gripped on to the cold steel of the bridge and glared at the scene of destruction. 'They'll pay!'

The fuel oil spreading over the water caught fire.

Men trying to swim in that lake of fire screamed and thrashed. They could not breathe. The skin of their faces and hands burned and peeled and crisped. Horrors screamed and thrashed in the water.

A Norwegian boat attempted to take up survivors; but the ferocity of the flames drove her back.

U-45 lay off.

There was nothing anyone could do now.

Dark heads showed among the flames of the burning oil. Hair frizzled and flashed. Eyes bubbled. Faces were stripped away to blackened skulls.

'You see?' said Forstner, vindictively. 'It was useless for us to turn back.'

Wolz could not refrain from spitting out a vicious comment.

'Had we turned back at once we could have saved some of those poor devils before the sea caught alight.'

Blucher listed still further, a dark bulky mass surrounded by a sea of flame.

The noise screeched on and on. Wolz turned away from Forstner, not caring for the idiot's reactions to his hot-tempered words, feeling the agony of the men in the blazing water. Now they were pitifully few. The cruiser heeled more and more, turning over, rolling to her grave.

She went quickly at the end. Her bows went down and, upside down, her stern flaunting, she slid beneath the waters.

Her rudder and screws looked pathetic, affixed to her hull, gaping blindly to the dull sky. The snow-flecked hillside beyond looked close, so close, as the ship sank. She was gone to a ship's tomb, to a Valhalla in the country of Valhalla, and a thousand men went with her.

'We should have gone straight in.' Forstner's lips were spittle-flecked. His face shone with a greenish tinge to the whiteness. 'Any opposition must be ruthlessly crushed. Surprise is all-important.'

He sounded distraught, as though he was quoting.

Wolz glimpsed something of the fear in the man.

'So there were other orders,' he said. He spoke stiffly.

'Of course! We are to strike and without question. Any opposition is to be smashed at once.'

It all made sense now.

Forstner shouted down to the quartermaster and U-45 began to turn, away from the spreading burning oil, and the smoke and the blackened hideous corpses of burned men.

'We must continue to carry out our orders.' Forstner spoke crisply, as though he had witnessed horror and pushed it from his mind. 'We did all we could. No one can blame us now.'

The lookout yelled before Wolz could answer.

'Man in the water! Off the port bow – swimming, but he's dead if we don't get to him.'

'Stop both engines,' shouted Wolz. 'Deck party, get down there and fish him out. Jump!'

The men tumbled down on to the casing. Lines were flung. The man in the water just had strength to grasp the loop and slip it over his shoulders. Then, like a lump of meat, he was dragged inboard.

The crewmen handled him as carefully as they might; but he was suffering. Wolz looked into his face as he was drawn up to the bridge to be passed down the conning tower hatch. The man's face showed ridged bone, tautly-stretched skin, wide and staring eyes that had looked on horror. He wore the remnants of a jacket that bore no military cut Wolz could recognise; the garment was in rags, the left shoulder was ripped away and the edges of the dark blue cloth were charred. The man's shoulder showed a mere pudding of black and red, a nauseous mess of burned flesh.

The man bumped into the periscope standard as he was being manoeuvred around to be passed feet first down the hatch.

'Careful!' bellowed Wolz. His face made the crewmen jump. 'Handle the poor chap gently – you can see he's in agony.'

The crewmen shuffled around, betraying a lively notion of what would happen if they displeased Oberleutnant z.S. Baldur Wolz.

Wolz bent over the survivor before he went down the hatchway. The man's shoulder looked a mess. His eyes held that haunted look of horror. Wolz guided his other shoulder gently, steering him down the hatch. He looked into the ravaged, haunted face.

'You're safe now,' said Wolz. 'You'll be all right now, my friend. The sanitatsobermaat will patch you up and we'll get you to a hospital right away. Now rest easy, if you can.'

The man's face showed no recognisable expression. But the two pallid worms that were his lips writhed and moved.

'Thank – you – ' The words were barely audible.

The ravaged hulk slid below to the tender mercies of Reche. Wolz turned back to the bridge rail as another hail went up. This time the man was in much better shape. He was S.S. – you could tell that even though his once-smart uniform was torn and bloodied and burned almost beyond recognition – and he came out much more smartly. He gasped and water poured from him. The strong stench of fuel oil hung in the air.

Macabre shadows danced across the waters as the oil burned; but this S.S. man had been lucky.

Wolz passed him below with a crisp: 'Glad we were able to pull you out. Get below and the sanitatsobermaat will look after you.'

At Wolz's elbow Forstner jerked and pointed; but the S.S. man spoke in a voice that brought the commander and the first lieutenant of U-45 around as one man.

'I demand – ' began the S.S. officer.

'You,' shouted Forstner, 'demand nothing! I am in command here. Get below. There are other survivors and you are in the way here. Get below!' And then, oddly, the Kapitänleutnant added: 'We may have to dive at any moment.'

That, of course, was a threat no landman could ignore.

The S.S. officer favoured Forstner with a look of incredible fury; but he had the sense not to argue.

Wolz, leaning over the hatch, said: 'It is a bit thick up here, Hauptsturmführer. But you're safe now. Get some coffee into you and get those burns seen to. We'll look after you.'

The S.S. Hauptsturmführer did not deign to say thank you. Instead, he said: 'That man – who is he?'

'The commanding officer of U-45. Now, please, get below. We have other casualties coming aboard.'

And Wolz turned away to cut the unnecessary conversation short.

Five other survivors were picked up and, although all were injured, all, Wolz considered, had a good chance of pulling through their ordeal alive.

Not so the next man.

He lay sluggishly in the water, almost drowned. Redness drifted from his lower parts. He was alive – just. But Wolz could see quite clearly that he was dying and that in five minutes at the most he would be dead. In all probability he had no idea what was happening, and his sluggish movements were all purely instinctive, just on the threshold of unconsciousness.

The damage done to his body sickened Wolz. Probably he had been caught in the explosion of the magazine and been hurled metres through the air. Then the blazing oil had finished the deadly work. His injuries were beyond succour.

Lindner on the casing forward threw a looped line.

The loop landed neatly about the casualty's extended arm and a trick of the waves drew it along past the wrist.

'He is the last,' shouted Forstner. 'Hurry with him, Cox'n.'

Lindner hauled on the rope, for the man was completely beyond helping himself.

The rope tightened. It looped the arm. The wet rope

gleamed through the water. Lindner hauled in. The survivor's arm ripped off where burns had eaten through under the shoulder. The man's body rolled over, the armless shoulder stumping up like a rotten tree-trunk drifting in an eddy. Lindner let out a yell as the rope splashed towards him, towing the severed arm. Blood spread murkily in the water.

'Hurry, man!' shouted Forstner.

'Leave him,' said Wolz in a voice as chill as the snow fields about them. 'He is almost dead. Let the poor devil die in peace.'

'But, sir,' said Lindner, looking up, the rope limp in his fingers, completely uncertain.

'Would you like to be tortured by being hauled up on to the casing, dragged on the steel, with your insides falling out? With your burned arms and legs falling off? Look at him, damn you, look at him! He's dead.'

'Wolz!' said Forstner. 'We can't leave a man – '

'He's hardly a man any longer. In seconds he will be dead. Let him die in peace.'

There appeared to Wolz no other course to follow. But he saw Forstner's face, and a breeze of alarm made him turn back to look at the man in the water. He had been a seaman, and what was left of him indicated he'd been a big man, full of blood, fleshy.

Speaking very calmly and yet making each word precise, Wolz said: 'Beg to report that the man is now dead, Herr Kapitänleutnant.'

Forstner let out a sigh.

Lindner, on the casing, swung up and opened his mouth to say something – Wolz had seen the last limp flopping of the casualty's remaining hand and so could guess what the P.O. would say – and so Wolz shouted, loudly: 'Secure all that raffle! Stand by for flooding.'

'Very good!' bellowed back Lindner.

At least, reflected Wolz, the P.O. understood what it was all about.

The deck party climbed to the bridge and then dropped smartly down the ladder. Wolz turned to Forstner.

'Do you wish me to clear the bridge for diving?'

Forstner put a hand to his lips.

'Dive? Why should we dive?'

'You told the S.S. Hauptsturmführer you wished to dive.'

'Well, what I tell the S.S and what I tell you, Wolz, are two different things. We will run up to Oslo as ordered.'

'Very good!'

As though dimly aware of some of the complexities of life in the Third Reich, some ten minutes later Forstner spoke in his habitual sharp manner to his first officer.

'Wolz! You had better go below and check the casualties. Make sure they are being cared for. Send Meyer up here.'

Wolz nodded and swung over into the hatch and slid down the steel ladder.

Engineer Officer Loeffler turned his broad squashed nose upwards.

'You're sending down a miserable bunch, Baldur. Has the commander any more for us?'

'No, thank God. That's all.' Then Wolz, reflecting that the crewmen of U-45 at their action stations within the steel coffin of the pressure hull hungered for news of events aloft, added: 'They sank *Blucher*, Chief. Terrible mess, burning. She must have lost a lot of men.'

Wolz was fully aware of what he was saying, although even to him the reality had not really altered his awareness. The war was the war. Ships were sunk. Men were killed. But *Blucher*, a wonderful cruiser of superb appearance and power, gone, burned and sunk – it was almost beyond credence.

'The talkative one's S.S.,' said the Chief.

'Yes. I had noticed.'

'Maybe they lost more than seamen, then.'

'Probably.'

Inane conversation to cover the deep wounds. The Kriegsmarine was desperately short of ships. Every one lost was like having a leg amputated, like that poor devil's arm being ripped off, burned through, rotten, dangling...

Wolz pushed through the control room and ducked through the open watertight doorway into the wardroom. The place gave him a sudden overwhelming sense of security, of normalcy, of rightness, despite its functional simplicity and the maze of piping and dangling parcels of food. The officer survivors had been brought in and laid out. Sanitatsobermaat Reche bent above the badly injured man. He turned as Wolz entered.

Before anyone else could speak the S.S. officer stumbled forward, hand outstretched. His face revealed feelings of deep importance to him. Wolz listened, his own face immobile.

'Do you realise what those murdering Norwegians have done? They have fired on the German flag! They have murdered German officers! Well, they'll rue the day once we are in control in Oslo, I can promise you.'

He shook with the emotions besetting him, exhaustion, fear, pain, all conspiring to betray him in the eyes of Baldur Wolz.

'You are being looked after?'

'What? Oh, yes, yes. The orderly treated me well enough. But we shall take Oslo. They cannot stop us. The parachutists will soon settle the business.

'Parachutists?'

The S.S. man sneered.

'You did not think we would leave an operation of this importance solely to the Navy, did you? The Luftwaffe will be tearing the heart out of them. Parachutists will be dropping on Fornebu. As soon as the airport is in our hands more troops will land. Then –'

Wolz considered. 'So we can continue on up the fjord? What you are saying means we can go on up?'

'Of course.'

'The aerodrome at Fornebu is the key point?'

'More or less. We must lay hands on the King and the government. This fellow Quisling is only a puppet. The King will command respect from his countrymen. We must put him into safe custody and then he will do as we say.'

Wolz realised the S.S. man was telling him this without realising what he was saying. He had been far more shattered by his experience than he realised, than his condition indicated. Wolz listened, fascinated.

The story was simple. A quick, bold thrust. Military bands. Parachutists and mountain troops, heavy tanks, quick striking columns. The Navy must be got out of the trap of the fjords before the British could react. Then the S.S. Hauptsturmführer's face clouded.

'But we have had too many reports of those damned British submarines sinking our tankers and supply ships. They were sent a few days ago, to be in readiness, sent under cover of innocent shipping. And the British are sinking them with their filthy submarines.' He glared at Wolz as though he hated all submariners.

'The British are good submariners,' said Wolz. 'But I am given to understand that their U-boats are inferior to ours.'

'One day, and soon,' said the S.S. Hauptsturmführer, 'we shall march against England. That will be The Day.'

Wolz was far too polite, far too busy, and far too cagey to mention the indelicate fact that the English Channel lay between the white cliffs of England and the marching jackboots of the Wehrmacht.

He did say, with a repression of that curious mixture of elation and depression he felt on these occasions, 'It will be a matter for the Kriegsmarine, then, I fancy.'

'Oh, the Navy will convey us.'

Wolz nodded, a little stiffly, and went on to bend over Reche's shoulder. The infernal arrogance of the fellow! He talked of the Navy as though the Kriegsmarine was a mere ferryboat service.

Reche glanced up.

'This one's in a bad way. That shoulder needs hospital attention.'

'We'll be in Oslo soon. We'll rush him to hospital as soon as we dock. Meanwhile, do what you can.'

The S.S. officer's hectoring voice rode over Reche's.

'I insist on seeing the commanding officer of this boat.' He made for the door leading to the control room. 'I shall go up and speak to him at once.'

'Hold on,' snapped Wolz. He strode back, ducking his head to avoid Loeffler's sausages. 'No one goes on to the bridge without authority.' Relenting a little, he added: 'If we have to dive suddenly we don't want bodies cluttering the upper deck.' And, then, unrelenting, a little maliciously, he finished: 'If you're not a U-boat man and you're on deck and we have to crash dive, you might get left. That would not be nice.'

The S.S. Hauptsturmführer half-turned, his head already ducked and his hands outspread to pass through the doorway.

'What is your name?'

'Oberleutnant zur See Wolz.'

'I am S.S. Hauptsturmführer Stahler. I outrank you. You would do well to moderate your tone.'

'I was merely giving you good advice, on the one hand, and, on the other, advising you of Naval procedure. No one goes on to the bridge without permission. No one.'

'Well, send the commander to see me. And find me some decent clothes.'

He gestured distastefully down his ruined field grey tunic. The twisted black and aluminium cording had been ripped from patches and collar and hung in a bedraggled mess. Most of the four aluminium buttons were missing, and the cloth itself was scorched, water-soaked, and miserable. His breeches were almost entirely absent. Wolz did not smile.

'Most of the clothing in a U-boat is permanently wet,' he said. 'But I will see what can be done. Once we are in Oslo – '

'Once we are in Oslo I shall know how to conduct myself.'

Wolz nodded. He said to himself, in English: 'Indubitably!'

That, as always, made him smile, cheered him up.

He went through the control room and bellowed up for permission to go topside. Meyer's thin voice screeched down.

When Wolz climbed through the tower up into the bridge and took a look around the snow-flecked hillsides of the fjord sliding away aft, the water looked just as cold, and all sight of *Blucher*'s death had passed away. Even the smoke was no longer visible.

'This S.S. chap,' he said carefully to Forstner. 'He sends his compliments, thanks us for pulling him out, and requests you will go down and speak to him. He has something to tell you, it seems.'

'He either does or he does not,' snapped Forstner. 'Not it seems he does.'

'Yes, of course.'

'Very well. I'll go down. Keep a sharp lookout. These Norwegians have tasted blood. If they start anything else our orders are to strike hard and ruthlessly. There can be no mistake. I shall hold you personally responsible, Wolz.'

'Very good.'

'Remember. For the moment we're in a shooting war.'

'I shall not forget.'

'Make it so.'

As Forstner began to descend the hatch, Wolz said, casually, he hoped casually enough: 'By the way. His name is S.S. Hauptsturmführer Stahler. He is not S.S.-V.T.'

'Oh.' That halted Forstner. 'So he's the real S.S.?'

'If you can call it real. Yes, that is so.'

Forstner said no more and disappeared down the conning tower. Wolz turned back to the bridge and took some satisfaction in barking at Meyer to keep the lookouts on the alert.

He shouldn't have made that last remark to Forstner. It was foolish. But, his cousin Siegfried, himself an S.S. officer, always made the distinction. Also, Siegfried had said that, as an S.S. Sturmbannführer and equivalent to a Wehrmacht major and moving up in the hierarchy himself, he could see ahead a little way into the future.

Cousin Siegfried would admit that he was a little privileged, also, in information. There was a time coming, he would say in his heavy way, when the S.S. would have to shoulder a great deal more of the burden of actually fighting this war. They would have to form field divisions, and parachute formations, and panzer corps. It was a necessity and was fully supported by the desires of the Führer. Those desires were apt to be fulfilled.

'You see, Baldur, we in the S.S. will have to police the new lands that will become our responsibility. After the war when we have won and fought in the field, then, as the Führer himself says in private, we will have the real authority to carry out our duties as state police.'

'So the Wehrmacht really has nothing to fear, then?' Wolz said. He and Siegfried were spending the morning fishing one of the estate's lakes where carp were supposed to be found. They had cast and cast and their rods looked very elegant; but they had so far caught nothing. It was a moment of quietness when confidences might be exchanged.

'You know what the Führer says about the Armed Forces? Of course you do.' Siegfried adjusted the set of his rod with a fussy little pantomime that would not hook more carp – if there were any there at all. 'The Führer says: "I have a National Socialist Luftwaffe, a Reactionary Army and a Christian Navy." So, you see...'

'I have heard it expressed a little differently.'

'Oh, yes, there are other versions. "Imperial" for instance. But the meaning is plain. He thinks of the Luftwaffe with our fat friend at its head as being totally loyal to the new Germany. The Army is suspect. He will use it to fight, of course, for that is what it is trained for and that is its function. But it is to the S.S. the Führer looks for true loyalty in that area.'

'I suppose so. But a Christian – or Imperial – Navy?'

Siegfried did not laugh; but he stroked a hand across his mouth, half-turning to Wolz. A fish jumped; but too far off to make out.

'He has no faith in the Navy. You know that. Raeder is a nonentity compared with Himmler, or even with Göring.'

'I suppose I should feel uncomfortable. But I do not. But Dönitz, now. He is no nonentity.' And here Wolz warmed to the subject. 'He knows that the U-boats can win the war. The U-boats can. We can starve England out and bring her to her knees.'

'That is what you say. But it will need the ground forces to impose the victory.'

'And the S.S-V.T. will provide those forces?'

'The S.S.-V.T. will provide the élite formations, Baldur.'

'Well, I hope you will pardon my saying so, but any victory of land or air forces will be carried on the previous victories of the U-boats. That, I passionately believe.'

Siegfried tilted his head. 'You and your U-boats, Baldur. I cannot understand how you can stick them. I'm told the smell is enough to make a man sick.'

'Yes. Sometimes. But one becomes accustomed to it.'

'You were lucky to be picked up on your last patrol, from what you tell me.'

'Oh,' said Wolz, twitching his rod up and fingering the line, ready to cast again, his eyes on a juicy patch of water just past a clump of reeds. He'd have to be careful to drop the bait just beyond and then let it glide gently just so . . . 'Oh, yes. Lucky. I'd quite given myself up for lost.'

He'd not told all the story, of course. He'd given no numbers of the U-boats involved. And, most certainly not, he had made no mention of the Bachstelze. There were, after all, on Dönitz's explicit instructions, secrets about the U-boat arm that must not be revealed.

'I was in the water when the U-boat surfaced right by me. I was lucky. I admit that. The experience has liberated me. I felt then and I feel now as though I was dead and have been reborn.'

Whether or not Cousin Siegfried knew what he was talking about, Baldur Wolz did not know. But, for himself, he would not easily forget falling from the Bachstelze, seeing U-42 submerging beneath him, and then hitting the water and seeing only the vast expanse of hostile ocean all about him. No, he wouldn't forget that in a hurry.*

And here he was, on leave, ostensibly recuperating after his ordeal. U-40 had picked him up and they'd loosed an eel at *Ark Royal*. It seemed they had not, after all, sunk her, and the British Aircraft carrier was still afloat. But, he felt with some comfort, a U-boat would get her in the end.

Admiral Dönitz had restricted all U-boat activity, and

* (See Sea Wolf Book 1. *Steel Shark*)

despite the end of season fishing he was half-enjoying himself on leave. Something big was brewing for the end of March. He'd been given this leave to recuperate – absolutely vital to be fully fit and healthy to endure the life in a U-boat, and that was no mere lip-service, no joke, it was a deadly fact of life beneath the sea – and been promoted Oberleutnant, which was gratifying. He hoped to be sent to a Type IX, as U-42 had been, and catch a long patrol. He did not particularly wish to go to a Type II and be stuck on short patrols around the coasts. Of course, the chances were he'd find himself in a Type VII for they were, after all, the most numerous class of U-boats.

U-42 had finally reached base safely. He had heard no more of the condition of her commander, Kapitänleutnant Gustav Ludecke. Ludecke's head wound had changed the man. Wolz made no particular efforts to keep in touch, although he sent a letter to Willi Weidman inviting him to stay when their leaves coincided. That made him think of Rudi.

The thought of his friend Rudi von Falkensbach made him frown. Rudi, a tremendous character, and still as harum-scarum as they'd been together as midshipmen, had been made up to Oberleutnant, done his Periscope School, and was, so he had written with all the infectious enthusiasm that communicated itself in the large sprawling handwriting from the crested notepaper flinging an immediate picture of him vividly before Wolz's eyes, about to be appointed commander. He'd get a Type II, a tiny craft of no more than 279 tons surfaced and 329 tons submerged. But Wolz's frown was occasioned not so much by the thought that Rudi was outstripping him. He was far more concerned that Rudi's recklessness would scupper him. He'd take his U-boat into scrapes that no thoughtful, methodical skipper would dream of allowing to happen to a refuse barge.

'What's the trouble, Cousin? The fish are not biting as one might wish; but . . . ?'

'I was thinking of Rudi. He'll do some rash, heroic deed and get himself depth-charged to perdition.'

Siegfried reeled in and looped his line, finger controlling neatly, cocking the rod, ready to cast.

'Oh, from what I hear he'll probably be posted to the Baltic to training duties. The flotillas up there always need instruction, or so I am told.'

Wolz put his rod down. He never really cared for fishing; but it was easier to go along than not. He made no comment on the curious sources of Siegfried's information. The S.S. had their white-gloved fingers in very many pies.

'He'll work-up in the Baltic, of course. But Rudi, being of the nobility, can still pull a few strings. He'll have himself sent on some hair-raising mission, for sure.'

'And you? Will you get your command soon?'

'I'd like to.'

My God! Was not that the understatement of the century? All Wolz hungered for in life, he often thought, was command of his very own U-boat. It would come. It had to come. If Rudi could do it, so could he. Even the thought of women paled – a little, a very little – in comparison.

As though reading his thoughts, Siegfried flicked his rod in with an air of finality, and said: 'They're not biting today. I think I shall take a walk over to the Hartstein place later on.'

'Trudi will be pleased to see you.'

Wolz, with a fatly satisfied inner feeling of joy, felt that to be a whopping lie.

Siegfried looked pleased at his cousin's words. He did not exactly smirk; but he licked his lips in a perfectly unconscious mannerism.

'Oh, yes, I think so, Baldur. She is a piece. I have very serious intentions there.'

'And Manfred?'

'My brother is a lunatic Luftwaffe pilot! He has no chance. If he doesn't kill himself in a crash he's just as likely to smash himself up. Trudi wants a man.'

Wolz bent and began packing his fishing gear. There was a huge outstanding matter between him and Trudi, the daughter of the Baroness von Hartstein. He had not as yet gone across to see her. But he would. He did not think Siegfried, or Manfred, would relish that knowledge; but he was warmed up and so prepared to risk their displeasure. Anyway, Trudi knew her own mind.

As always – as damnably always – his thoughts shied away from Cousin Lisl. Now, if only she...

He'd been singularly fortunate that his aunt and uncle had taken him in when his mother died soon after his father had gone down in his U-boat. They'd treated him well. He was one of the family. And, ironically enough, against all the hoary traditions, he got on well with his cousins and liked them and they, to their credit, liked him also. He had made not a single move towards Lisl. He just didn't dare...

A strange, odd, almost frightening attitude for a hairy U-boat man who raced through girls with all the zest of a sailor off a windjammer around the Horn in the stews of Hamburg.

Packing up their traps, Siegfried made a last, almost dismissive comment on the Navy.

'I have heard – this is privileged information, Baldur, and so do not repeat it – I have heard that the Führer, with the reluctant consent of Raeder and the Navy chiefs, has cancelled the Fleet Programme. We are to have no more huge battleships and cruisers.'

'Maybe. I feel sorry for that. But the U-boat Programme will go ahead and increase.'

'Of course. You're cheap and expendable.'

'I don't regard myself as expendable in that sense. And I'm not cheap! You heard the announcement of the First of March! Your fat friend's Luftwaffe has sunk 36,000 tons of shipping so far. The surface ships have sunk 63,000. And 281,000 tons have been sunk by mines. But – '

'I know.'

'Yes! We U-boat men have sunk 750,000 B.R.T.! Now you can't say we're not winning the war for Germany!'

'It's a lot, I'll agree. But we have to sink a lot more. We have to do better.'

Wolz picked up his rod and gear and started for the schloss. He did not say 'And how much have the S.S. sunk?' for there was a perfectly commonsense and reasonable answer to that. But the thought simmered in his mind.

He did say, in an even voice: 'At the moment, through force of circumstances, it is only the Navy who are fighting the war against England.'

'That will change, and soon.' Then Siegfried strode on ahead, and Wolz was left with the tantalising impression that his S.S. cousin knew a great deal more than he was saying.

Well, as Wolz conned U-45 up Oslofjord, he could not be in any doubt that Cousin Siegfried knew what he had been talking about – or, rather, what he had not talked about.

This descent upon Norway, which had been billed as a friendly attempt to protect the Norwegians from the perfidious English, was looking more and more as though it was a case of the Germans jumping in first. On principle, Baldur Wolz was all for that. Whatever the machinations behind the scenes, whatever had gone on in the Chancelleries of the Powers involved, one thing was patently obvious: the long naked coastline of Norway was of enormous strategical importance. Whoever held that in the struggle held an ace. If the English established bases there, put out air patrols, used their deadly destroyers from the handy anchorages – why, the U-boat arm might never break through to the fat pickings of the Atlantic.

And, if the English could be kept out, if the Germans could set up their own bases here, why, then the U-boats would knock a thousand miles off their passages to and from the areas of action. The advantage to the U-boats would be so immense that almost any risk was worth taking to secure these tempting naval bases.

So Baldur Wolz reconciled himself through the good of Germany to a strict obedience to his orders.

Ahead, the snow-spattered hillsides trended away as the fjord widened to the headland on the starboard side. The sounds of aeroengines drifted down. The airfield of Fornebu lay ahead, and if the Stukas were going to plaster that, the Norwegians had best stand from under. The distant sounds came muffled. The overcast prevented any clear sightings. Just in case any Norwegian aircraft put in an appearance, Wolz kept an alert lookout aloft. The Norwegians had bought Gloster Gladiator fighters from England. Old and antiquated though the biplanes might be, they could still stitch a string of machine gun bullets across the open bridge of a U-boat.

'Aircraft coming in from astern!' bellowed the stern lookout.

Wolz span about.

For a moment, his mind occupied with the characteristic outlines of a Gladiator, he failed to register just what he was seeing.

Instead of the biplane wings, and the compact rugged look of an interceptor, he saw a wide-winged aeroplane, her three propellers churning, her tall tail clearly visible. He saw the swastikas even as he realised what a fool he was – she was an old Iron Annie. Of all aeroplanes in the whole wide world to mistake!

'Hold your fire!' he rasped. That too, was unnecessary; but Wolz intended to take no stupid chances, not while he held the bridge.

The Junkers Ju 52/3m banked away, her corrugated skin glistening, swerved a little drunkenly to port. She was off course for Fornebu. Even as Wolz watched, the transport continued her turn, banking away, her wings wide and angular against the dull overcast. She reversed course and headed back down the fjord.

'What's the fool playing at?' said Meyer, aggressively.

Wolz ignored him.

'Keep your eyes skinned on the fjord,' he rasped at the lookouts. Two of them had been gawping aloft.

They swung back to their stations and Wolz, too, took a long sweep around the circle of water. The headland cut off the forward starboard section and, again as he was staring thoughtfully at the water beyond, seeing the peculiar colours and strata of lights and shadows there, a sharp black prow headed around the land. A steep white bow-wave cut back. He saw the low lean grey shape, the fume of funnel smoke, the hurtling aggressive hunter steaming at top speed straight for U-45. The gun barked angrily from the foredeck. A 10 centimetre gun, snapping out harshly, sending a spray of water across the U-boat's casing.

Meyer was screaming: 'Destroyer! Destroyer!'

Wolz saw the whole picture in a single all-encompassing grasp of imagination.

The jager speeding towards them across the water would ram them broadside on, cut them down, roll them over.

'Destroyer!' shrieked Meyer, distraught. And then the fool shouted: 'We must dive! Flood! Flood!'

'No!' bellowed Wolz. 'Belay that, you idiot! Quartermaster, steer nine-oh! Full ahead both! Herr Leutnant Meyer, if I hear another order out of you before I give you leave I'll have you shot!' And then, down the voicepipe again: 'Chief! Give me everything you've got!'

As U-45 turned hard astarboard, so the jager bore down on her at a full thirty knots, aiming to ram and sink.

CHAPTER SIX

The hard sharp prow lanced through the water at them. The white upswept bow wave foamed like a banner. U-45 began to turn, agonisingly slowly to Wolz, gripping the conning tower metal until his knuckles threatened to burst. He stared with fascinated intensity on the destruction hurtling down on the labouring U-boat.

He knew the destroyer, he had recognised her instantly in the first flashing glimpse as she swept out of her ambush. The Norwegians knew the Germans were coming. This jager had waited with steam up, building her speed at the right moment until at the crucial second she had burst from her concealment to tear down at thirty knots, prepared to ram and rend, to smash and destroy.

U-45 came around. Wolz held on. He knew the Norwegian vessel from long study of the Navies of the world. She was a jager, of the Sleipner class, not quite a real destroyer, more of a torpedo boat. But she had teeth. Her 10 centimetre gun spat again and the shell smacked into the water close alongside the U-boat's saddle tank. Wolz watched the splash and the waterspout impassively. The jager bore on. She displaced only 597 tons, to be sure; and although U-45 displaced 753 tons on the surface, the impact would be a tremendous shock for both vessels.

'Come on!' said Wolz, and he let go the steel rail and hammered with his fist. 'Come *on!*'

Loeffler had cranked his diesels into full revolutions, impelled by the urgency of Wolz's orders. U-45 turned, heeling over, cutting through the water, bringing her bows on to the approaching jager.

Now Wolz saw the bows of U-45 line up with the bows of the oncoming jager.

The two vessels sped through the water directly at each other.

Wolz made no attempt to dive. Long before they could have slid below the surface the jager would be on them, slashing into their plating, sending them to the bottom.

Seconds only had passed.

'You madman!' screamed Meyer. He showed a shocked, green-tinged white face to Wolz, and then he dived for the open rear of the bridge. He leaped out on to the steel deck of the wintergarden, hustling the men there. He blundered on. Before he could reach the deck the two vessels struck.

Clinging on, Wolz felt the collision as a stupendous upheaval of all the world.

He caught fragmentary glimpses. The sharp prow of the jager lancing down, and the squat bows of U-45 biting in. Of the forward hydroplane, upreared, being wrenched away. Of the long tearing scream of metal. A massive chunk ripped free of the jager's plating. The Norwegians had not rammed a defenceless U-boat in flank; they had been met by a bull-headed frontal charge. They, in their turn, had been rammed.

The noise screeched like a madman's kettledrum in hell. Bits of metal flew. The two ships upreared together, like praying mantises slashing madly one at the other. Then the Norwegian fell off to starboard and U-45 fell off on the other side. With a manic clanging of ripping metal and shrieking steel, the two ships passed down each other's flanks.

Steam gushed from severed pipes. U-45 was surging

uncontrollably. Wolz clung to the bridge with both fists gripped into knots. His head rang with the concussion.

U-45 rolled deeply. She shuddered. He could hear all kinds of diabolical noises spurting up from below, the sounds of smashing and destruction down there as everything was torn loose. God knew what he'd done to the boat's guts.

He retained a vague impression of seeing the jager sliding alongside. He'd heard a fierce chattering. Now he saw one of the lookouts – it was Gerhard Freydank – slide slowly to the deck. His face twisted up, foolishly. The machine gun bullet had made a small hole in his forehead. As Freydank rolled limply over, the back of his head came into view. Only his head had no back. The bullet had torn away a great chunk of skull, and blood and brains oozed greasily.

Wolz put a hand to his head and felt the wet tackiness there. When he looked at his fingers they were red with blood.

He must have been hit, a crease along the forehead, if that was not Freydank's blood spattered over him.

He didn't know, and right at this moment it was not important.

He could still function.

'Stop both engines,' he croaked down the voicepipe. 'Report damage. Close up gun's crew. *Jump!*'

The jager was swerving in the water, listing badly, but coming around, and already her 10 centimetre was shooting. They were not making good practice over there; the first shell went nowhere. But in a moment or two they'd have the range.

The gun's crew tumbled out. They looked dazed.

'Get that flak going!' bellowed Wolz. 'Hurry! He'll damage us in a second – knock out his guns! *Jump!*'

The gun's crew clustered around the 8.8 centimetre and the ready-use ammunition was passed up. The hatch over the magazine in the passageway by the wardroom would be flung open now and the men would be handing up the rounds. The 8.8. snouted around. Wolz refrained from yelling any more orders, for the men on the gun knew what to do and they were trained to shoot straight.

The 2 centimetre flak opened up in a long ripping burst.

Down there Meyer was looking about frantically, one hand bent over his head.

'Get up here, Herr Leutnant Meyer!' shouted Wolz. 'You have your duty to do – so damn well do it!'

Meyer mewed and fell down. His legs twitched. Wolz decided to let him stay there as an object lesson, and guessed he was probably doing the wrong thing and would no doubt regret it later – if there was a later.

Kapitänleutnant Adolf Forstner appeared on the bridge. His thin face held a dangerous flush. His eyes were brighter than Wolz remembered them as having been for some time.

'What the hell's going on, Wolz? What have you been doing to my command?'

'Beg to report we have a fight on our hands,' said Wolz, crisply and with some enjoyment.

At that precise moment a shell from the jager cracked off close into the water. Spray slashed inboard. Forstner received a good bucketful across the face. Wolz was not splashed. And they said the gods did not differentiate!

'Why don't you dive, Wolz?' Forstner glared about at the chaos. Smoke whipped back from the guns. Men were dragging wounded comrades away from interference with rapid fire. The jager fired again and the howl of the shot passed perilously close.

'Dive?' said Wolz. 'Oh, we've lost our forward port hydroplane, we're probably messed up below – and that fellow over there has depth charges and he'll see us go down, and then – poof!'

Forstner sniffed.

Wolz could smell it too.

A head appeared in the hatchway, a blunt head with a fierce red beard and a broad flattened nose. Loeffler's face was scarlet, his eyes ran, and he coughed.

'You'll have to get 'em all up,' he said. 'You can't breathe down there.'

'Everybody on deck,' said Wolz. 'On the double.'

'But . . . ' said Forstner.

'The collision has cracked some cells of the batteries – just how many cells is academic. If the pressure hull is punctured and sea water gets in . . .'

'You do not need to tell me, Wolz.'

The men started to scramble up through the conning tower.

Wolz looked at the jager. She had not fired when he'd expected her to.

She was leaning over, listing more and more, and he saw the long ugly gash torn in her side by U-45 was slipping beneath the water.

'She's done for. So we can chalk up more tonnage.'

'And we are, too, you bungler! You should have dived!'

Wolz flared up at that, and he only just caught himself in time. Forstner was more than a simple idiot; he was a dangerous idiot.

'I have already told you. If we'd dived we'd be down there now and we'd never have come up.'

'And now?'

Wolz turned to Loeffler.

'Chief, is it possible to start the engines again? I want to run us aground.'

'Of course.'

Loeffler spoke as though it was the most natural thing in the world. He waited while the S.S. Hauptsturmführer, loudly complaining, hoisted himself up through the conning tower hatch. Wolz saw.

'Break open the other hatches,' he said. 'Get some air through. And you can cease fire.'

The mad yammer of the 2 centimetre died. The gun's crew had gone on firing; but now all could see the Norwegian jager was doomed.

'They're getting boats over,' said Wolz. 'Aye, and a raft too. They should be all right.'

'We are not going to their assistance, in any case,' snapped Forstner.

'As you order, Herr Kapitänleutnant.'

Forstner's face pinched in.

'Look out down below!' yelled Loeffler. The Chief swung into the hatch and slid out of sight. Wolz counted. He did not smile as the diesels picked up with a thump; but once again he felt reassurance that he was shipped out with a Chief of the calibre of Loeffler.

The narrow deck of U-45 crowded with men. Most had their lifejackets with them; but not all. Wolz saw how they eyed the water, and some, he fancied, were getting their nerves up to jump.

'Now listen to me!' he shouted, making them turn their heads to face him. 'There's no need to abandon ship. That water is cold! I know. We're going to beach in a nice orderly fashion. Then we can step ashore dry-shod.'

'What happened?' demanded Hauptsturmführer Stahler. Now everyone was looking across at the sinking Norwegian jager. She was rolling over. Steam and smoke burst from her. The water rolled away, greasy. The men in the boats and on the rafts paddled frantically.

'The ship you now see sinking, Hauptsturmführer, attempted to ram and sink us. But we got in our blow first. Now she's sinking. But we have to beach.'

'That gas down there – it'll burn my lungs out.'

'There is no gas at the moment, I assure you. The Chief is down there and if there was any chlorine about he'd be up here quicker than a rabbit with a ferret on its tail. Believe me.'

The S.S. officer did not look convinced.

U-45 rolled sluggishly and righted herself. She carried on on the same course Wolz had given the helmsman. There was need only to give a few final corrections to bring them to what appeared to be the only strip of beach along that sloping cliffside. The snow looked bleak and the prospect ahead not at all inviting.

But however tough the hours ahead might be, they were, as Wolz knew only too well, nothing compared with what would have happened had the jager sunk them in the fjord.

He bellowed for Lindner and when the P.O. appeared he said: 'Break out the small arms, cox'n and distribute them. I'll have an MP38, I think. We may arouse a little opposition among the locals.'

Meixner, who had taken over as the 2 centimetre flak gunner after poor Fischer's ghastly death, came up to say: 'We can unship the flak sir, and bring it along. Might be useful.'

'That's not a feather pillow you'll be lugging along, and the ammunition will pull the arms out of your sockets.'

'We'll manage, Herr Oberleutnant. You'll see.'

'A good idea,' said Forstner, brisking up, having a problem he fancied he could decide. 'Yes. Bring the flak, Fischer – it is Fischer, isn't it?'

'Meixner, Herr Kapitänleutnant.'

'Oh, Meixner. Yes, of course.'

Stubbornly, Wolz said: 'We have to cross the mountains – or hills, anyway. We have badly wounded men. With respect, I suggest it would be better to leave the flak where it is.'

Meixner looked hurt.

Forstner bit his thumb, turning away.

Wolz said: 'It's a good idea, Meixner. But it's not

practical in our situation. Now help with the wounded. And grab yourself a rifle. At least you can carry that when your feet are bleeding and your guts hurt.'

'Very good!'

U-45 glided gently in towards the scrap of beach.

'Stop both!'

'Stop both!'

'And come up on deck and get a breath of fresh air, Chief.'

Wolz cast a quick glance at Forstner. The commander stood with his hands on the rail, leaning over, as though in full command of the situation. He'd tacitly acquiesced in Wolz's handling of the situation. Now that was strange. Surely, he had some pride? But then, clearly, he was a man who knew the odds, how to play what he had; a man who would let his subordinates do the dirty work and take the credit. To any interrogator it would be all too simple to say, merely, that he had been in overall command and had given his orders for his first lieutenant to carry out. That was the usual style...

Wolz leaned out beside the commander and bellowed: 'Grab on to a good handhold and belay yourselves firmly. We're going to beach.'

U-45 hit with a rolling of shingle and the grating of metal. Wolz had judged it nicely. She slid up on to the beach, ripping away a great deal of her lower anatomy, no doubt, and ruining the valves of the saddle tanks; but she rolled gently to a stop with the water susurrating past her flanks. The men were jerked about only a little. The wounded were firmly braced up in their stretchers. All in all, decided Baldur Wolz, perhaps a little too smugly, a very nice piece of seamanship.

The stern floated free. U-45 began to swing.

Loeffler appeared on the bridge. He looked just as tough and competent; but he held a great oil-soaked swatch of cloth, and he coughed a little too heavily for Wolz's liking.

'Yes?' said Wolz. 'And what gave you the idea you were a hero? You should have come up before.'

'That's all the thanks, is it?' said Loeffler. He coughed and choked and spluttered.

'Where were we holed?'

'Right aft. A dinky little hole from the Norwegian's gun, I'd say. The chlorine was building up slowly; we'd never have stoppered that hole in time.'

Forstner looked agitated.

'There is chlorine?'

'That's what one gets when seawater and sulphuric acid get together in unholy matrimony. You don't need a chemist to tell you that.'

'I shall not forget your offensive remarks, Chief.'

'And I shall not forget the Chief who stayed at his post of duty,' said Wolz.

He bellowed in the general direction of the hands clustered on the deck awaiting orders.

'Directly you get on shore I want a scouting party out. Herr Leutnant Ehrenberger, take a party up to the top of that hill and report what you see. Get the wounded off first and treat them gently. Now, move!'

'Very good,' said Ehrenberger. The second officer jumped down on to the beach, plunging into the shingle. His MP38 banged his back. Lindner was second man ashore. Wolz turned to Forstner. 'You will, of course, be the last, Herr Kapitänleutnant. I shall see to the secret papers.'

'You forget yourself, Wolz! That is my job!'

Wolz nodded. He did not say: 'Well, do it!' But it was pretty clear cut.

S.S. Hauptsturmführer Stahler pushed forward aggressively.

'I demand a machine pistol! I understand what you Navy people do not!'

'Oh,' said Wolz. 'We sailors understand how to fight on land, never you fear. But you may have a weapon, of course, if that will please you.' During this interchange Forstner turned to the conning tower hatch. He paused. Stahler and Loeffler and Wolz regarded him gravely. The men were jumping ashore. They were treating the whole thing as a lark, now, now that danger of being sunk had gone.

For the smallest fraction of time, for less than a heartbeat, Forstner looked like a hunted and trapped animal.

Then – well, Baldur Wolz had to hand it to the commander.

Forstner turned away from the open hatch from which already the familiar stinks were subtly changing to a more lethal perfume, a stench of chemical horror dreaded by all U-boat men.

'I'll handle the Hauptsturmführer, Wolz. I can deal adequately with the S.S. on a basis of mutual respect. You go and do as you suggested.'

'I don't recall, what was that? I was about to set up a reconnaissance of that hill...'

'You know what I mean!'

Loeffler coughing, said: 'The secret papers, Baldur.'

'Oh!'

Forstner blustered on. 'I am particularly pleased that you volunteered for this task, Herr Oberleutnant. I shall not forget it in my report. Now, please hurry. The Norwegians will be ashore soon and I have no desire to be taken prisoner.'

Wolz looked across at the boats and rafts. They were headed for the beach, the boats towing the rafts.

He hefted the machine pistol Lindner had handed him.

'I do not think we shall be their prisoners,' he said.

The violence of his own feelings shook him, for just a moment. The idea of sitting out the war in a prisoner of war camp scared him more than most things could. He handed the MP38 to Loeffler. 'Hold on to this for me, will you, Chief? The fug shouldn't be too bad in the wardroom – and the captain's cabin.'

The last was a blatant dig. Forstner ignored it.

Wolz grabbed Loeffler's mess of wadded cloth and stepped across to the conning tower hatch.

He'd have to be quick. As his English friends used to say, Bloody Quick. Or, as Sub-lieutenant Richard Algernon Mitchell liked to phrase it: 'P.D.Q.!'

He took a deep gulping breath and slid feet first down the ladder. The stink was powerful. He hit the steel deck of the conning tower, slid on through to the control tower room without a pause. The fug was not too bad as yet. But the deadly build up of the chlorine would soon kill every last living thing in the pressure hull.

He could hear a distant slosh of water, and the grating of the boat on the shingle. It took him moments only to whip into the wardroom, rip the commander's green curtain away and smash out the secret papers. Next, the radio room, where codes and signal ciphers were perhaps not of the same importance but must, nevertheless, be prevented from falling into the hands of the enemy.

He caught a gagging breath of foul air and knew his time was up.

Up, up he had to go, with his arms full and the wadding cloth slipping from his nose and mouth. His head was bursting. He stuffed a mass of papers into the front of his leather jacket. The ladder felt cold and greasy under his fingers, the gloves ripped and shredded, an astonishing fact he had not noticed before.

Up, up he went.

When he stuck his head out into the cold fresh air, it was like plunging into the snow from a sauna.

'Come on, Baldur,' and Loeffler gripped under his armpits and hauled him out.

The papers bulged the front of his leather jacket and the rest fluttered under his arm. He gave a push to his cap to set it at the correct angle, slapped a salute that he felt to be wholly ironic, and said: 'Beg to report safe recovery of the secret papers and logs, Herr Kapitänleutnant.'

Forstner, not untypically of late, was at a loss for the correct words to speak. Finally he nodded, stiffly, and said: 'See they are destroyed in my presence, Wolz.'

'They're too damp to burn. There was no time for the weighted box.'

'Herr Oberleutnant,' said Hauptsturmführer Stahler. 'Here.' He handed across a linen handkerchief that was a marvel of whiteness and cleanliness. 'You are crying. I happened to have retained this handkerchief, luckily, it seems.'

Wolz's eyes stung so much he thought they must be exposed on stalks. He took the handkerchief – like everything else in a U-boat it was damp – and dabbed cautiously. The handkerchief had been scrounged by Ehrenberger for the S.S. Officer's use.

'Thank you,' said Wolz. 'It was pretty thick down there.'

Then, because he was Baldur Wolz and thoroughly fed up with this clot Forstner, as well as being extremely cautious about the S.S. man Stahler, he had to add: 'These tears, I assure you, are entirely on my own account.'

And S.S. Hauptsturmführer Stahler laughed.

CHAPTER SEVEN

After some initial confusion and reverses, the airfield at Fornebu was finally taken by the Luftwaffe. The heavy menacing cloud cover forced the return of the first wave of Junkers transports carrying the first two companies of parachutists. Second Group of the 1st Special Duty Wing were not, in the event, as experienced in bad weather flying as 2nd Special Duty Wing. Even so, it was a touch and go affair.

Gloster Gladiators of the Norwegian Air Force shot down four of the German aircraft. Following aircraft shied away. Later during the day, as U-45 sluggishly rolled in the fjord, fifty-three aircraft of the second wave were recalled because of the earlier failures.

The German attempt on Oslo had failed.

But Hauptman Wagner, leading that second wave, refused to believe the recall signal genuine and pressed on.

Weserubung hung in the balance.

The onslaught on Norway and Denmark, code-named Weserubung, rested at that moment on the slender hopes of two companies of troops successfully landing in face of opposition and then, somehow, being in the position to take the capital city of Oslo.

The moment Wagner's Ju52 came in to land he was killed by machine gun fire.

The crisis still sparked. Then eight Messerschmitt Bf110 fighters, desperately short of fuel, were forced to land at Fornebu. They came in expecting the worst, winging down over the airfield, tensing for the expected impact of bullets.

Nothing happened.

Startled, Oberleutnant Hanzen swiftly ordered the rear gunners of the twin-engined craft to cover the defences. The big planes peeled off and landed like vultures settling on a corpse. The crisis had been averted. The German air attaché, Hauptman Spiller, waiting in a fever of impatience for the arrival of German forces, could now greet them and brief them on the latest situation. There was little chance, now, of taking the king. The agents of the Gestapo had been in *Blucher*.

A headquarters assigned to Stavanger was re-routed, with typical German flexibility, to Oslo. The First Special Duty wing flew on from Aalborg where they had taken refuge from the bad weather. At half-past three, six companies were at last free to begin the march into the capital.

This was the moment for the military band.

Thumping and trumpeting away, marching with a swing, the band led the little force into Oslo, for all the world as though the whole of Norway was now a German province.

Weserubung had brilliantly succeeded.

The Luftwaffe attacked the Oskarsborg fortress with vicious intent, swooping in and dropping their bombs with all the old panache that had conquered Poland. But the ancient fortress was not so easily destroyed, and the Luftwaffe could do no more than impede the traverse of the guns by the mounds of ripped and blasted debris.

But this was enough.

Led by *Lutzow*, the Kriegsmarine ships could steam up the fjord and so enter Oslo.

No one seemed quite sure what to do with the crew of a U-boat left stranded. S.S. Hauptsturmführer Stahler had saluted formally, the stiffly extended right arm, thrust aggressively aloft, dark against the pallid sky.

'I thank you for what you have done, Herr Kapitänleutnant. I owe my life to you and your crew. Now I have my duties here.' He half-turned, still stiff, still at the salute. He faced Wolz. 'Thank you, Herr Oberleutnant. Heil Hitler!'

Gravely, Forstner and Wolz returned the salute, giving the formal Navy salute, their gloved hands to their caps.

'Heil Hitler!' snapped Forstner.

Stahler slapped his arm down, about faced, and marched off across the jetty where already the busy activity of naval working parties was first cluttering the piers and then swiftly clearing them for fresh shipments.

'I doubt if we'll see him again,' remarked Forstner. He sounded pleased.

'The question is, what do we do? The wounded to the hospital, of course. Find a radio and signal B.d.U.' Wolz eyed Forstner meanly. 'Herr Kapitänleutnant. With respect, I must point out that we cannot allow ourselves, as U-boat men, to become embroiled with the Wehrmacht or the Luftwaffe ground forces in the fighting.'

'I do not need you to tell me what to do. My command may for the moment be temporarily disabled. Our first job is to find salvage equipment. We must refloat her and fix the batteries –'

'Of course. But, again with respect, I must point out that we are likely to be treated with scant courtesy here. The admiral is missing. *Lutzow* is probably our best bet.'

'Exactly my thought. You'd better come with me. Tell Ehrenberger to carry on here.'

'Very good.'

As they made their way across the jetty towards the massive bulk of *Lutzow*, Wolz reflected that perhaps Forstner had tried to copper-bottom his bet in so speedily returning the S.S. man's Heil Hitler. There was not a lot of that in the Navy.

Major-General Engelbrecht, in command of 169th Division charged with taking Oslo, and Rear-Admiral Kummetz had been captured by the Norwegians after *Blucher* sank. They were among the lucky ones. The naval attaché had waited for the ships of Group Five in vain.

Now, as Wolz stepped up to *Lutzow*, he tried to take some comfort from the solidity of her, her bulk and evident power, despite the damage she had taken at the narrows.

The air of excitement infected everyone. Everybody seemed to be working in a tight, taut, pent-up condition, knowing how close to the wind they were sailing. Norway had to be taken. That was the imperative. The Navy had carried out its tasks brilliantly at the other selected points for landing. Oslo had proved the biggest nut to crack. But, and here Wolz mentally tipped his hat to Cousin Manfred, the Luftwaffe had pulled the chestnuts out of the fire here.

Soldiers of the 3rd Mountain Division were coming ashore from *Lutzow*, tough, wiry, competent men, with their special equipment giving them an advantage in the conditions the infantry were likely to meet. *Lutzow* had originally been scheduled to go in the Trondheim attack force, but her machinery had played up, so she had been switched to Oslo. That, now, was a blessing.

General Nikolaus von Falkenhorst commanded operation Weserubung, and he, Wolz knew, would be so busy planning his next moves that he and his staff would have no time for a U-boat crew without a U-boat.

'We must radio Dönitz,' he said to Forstner as they went below in *Lutzow*, to wait to make their report. 'We must look to the Navy and only the Navy. If once we're sucked into the land fighting –'

Forstner interrupted, sarcastically. 'What, Wolz? You

have no stomach for infantry fighting in the snow?'

Wolz shut his mouth, tightly, gripping with his jaws. Then, for the hell of it, he forced himself to relax and say: 'No.'

Forstner could make nothing of that.

The interview with the captain was short and relatively sweet. Permission was given to make a direct report to B.d.U. The radio facilities of *Lutzow* would be put at their disposal for the shortest possible time. Radio traffic was brisk. Anyway, the surface sailors looked a little askance on the U-boat men. They were not as bad as the Wehrmacht or the Luftwaffe or the S.S.; but, all the same, Wolz was left in no doubt that all U-boat men were considered as more than a little mad and a race apart.

B.d.U.'s reply was brisk and to the point.

'Report present status and readiness of crew.'

Forstner put his thumb in his mouth, caught Wolz's eye, and whipped it out, quickly.

Patiently, Wolz said: 'We are an effective U-boat crew. Fully operational. That is what matters. U-45 can be salvaged later. If we get the facilities.'

They concocted a reply.

The return signal made Forstner look dazed, and Wolz let his thin lips rick up in a smile. He did not laugh aloud, for the radio-operators had to be suitably impressed with U-boat men; but among his own kind he would have whooped with joy and flung his cap high into the air, completely abandoned to the glorious opportunity ahead. Forstner, it was clear, did not regard their orders in quite the same way.

Letting his guard slip for long enough to blurt out his thoughts, Forstner said: 'Hell and damnation! I was sure we'd be ordered back to Kiel.'

'U-55,' said Wolz. He rubbed his spread fingers over his beard stubble. 'U-51 was assigned to Narvik as well. I trust she survived the attack.'

Forstner snapped a fingernail at the signal form. His

actions were pettish, reflecting his own annoyance at his revealing words.

'It does not clearly say why the crew is unable to take the boat off themselves.'

'My guess is they're all dead. Or prisoners.'

'These Norwegians! They must be taught a lesson. Any resistance must be crushed.'

The Kapitänleutnant spoke as though reading a lesson learned by heart.

Deciding it was time to get moving, Wolz said: 'We have the remainder of our own rations; but I'll see if I can ferret out more. We'll need all we can get, going up to Narvik. I'll see what the Luftwaffe can do for us, as well.' He would have gone on speaking; but Forstner turned away.

'Make all the arrangements, Herr Oberleutnant, according to our orders. I have important business in Oslo. I shall meet you at Fornebu when the travel arrangements have been finalised.'

'The signal has been repeated to the Air Officer Commanding, and that must mean the Luftwaffe have agreed to provide an airlift for us. The arrangements – '

Again Forstner cut off his First Lieutenant in mid flight.

'Yes, of course! That is your responsibility, Herr Oberleutnant. Get the crew to Narvik. How you do it is your affair.'

'Very good!'

The Luftwaffe Hauptmann was a much harassed officer. He pushed his steel-rimmed glasses higher on his nose and moved a pile of papers from one side of the plank desk to the other. The sounds of typewriters echoed from the next room, past the feather-boarded partition, and Luftwaffe personnel were continually passing and re-passing. The air smelled of heat and sweat and frustration, and the pot-bellied iron stove stoked up the warmth.

'Impossible,' said the Luftwaffe Hauptmann, and scrawled a few unintelligible lines on a report and tossed it into the basket.

'But,' said Baldur Walz, leaning forward, speaking with great care, 'I have direct orders which have been agreed by the Luftwaffe –'

'Orders, my dear Herr Oberleutnant, are not aeroplanes.'

'I must get my crew to Narvik.'

The harsh electric light glinted ferociously on the steel frames. The Hauptmann looked as though he was confronted by a madman.

'Narvik? Haven't you heard what's going on up there?'

'No.'

The pen scratched again and a further paper changed baskets. The Hauptmann's face showed lines of fatigue and concern; that was none of Wolz's business.

'We ran into trouble – English destroyers. The details are garbled, understandably so, but a decision has been reached. We hold Narvik. How long we hold it, I gather, is up to the Luftwaffe.'

'I see what you mean. But my orders instruct me to report at Narvik. There is a U-boat there . . .' Wolz hesitated. The Luftwaffe man probably didn't give a damn about U-boats. Secrecy was important; but if he didn't get the crew to Narvik, secrecy would be unnecessary, for U-55 would not have a crew. There was no choice.

'This U-boat has been damaged but is still seaworthy. I must fly my crew up there. If there are English destroyers at work, then a U-boat is vitally necessary.'

Wolz kept a straight, serious face as he spoke. The situation was near enough desperate; but he knew that many an old U-boat hand would wonder what he meant.

U-boats and English destroyers made uncomfortable bedpartners.

The Luftwaffe officer was overtired, overworked, under a tremendous strain; but he was no fool.

'How did the U-boat get there in the first place? Why does its crew not sail it?'

Wolz spread his hands. The corners of his mouth turned down.

'The destroyers you mentioned . . . The crew were forced to abandon ship and were all either killed or captured. The Norwegians –'

'Ach! These Norwegians. We understand that Major Quisling would have them well in hand.'

'Do I get my two planes?'

'Two? You want two Tante Jus? The Geschwader is fully stretched and Second Group . . . You saw the field as you came in?'

Outside lay the shattered wrecks of Ju52s mingled with the Messerschmitt 110s and the Norwegian Gladiators. The place was a shambles, with working parties clearing up the debris and bringing order out of chaos, with the German aeroplanes landing and taking off through it all.

'I saw.'

'And, anyway, you can't land at Narvik. They're building a strip. I believe we may have to land on a lake. At Hartvigvatn.' He looked up sharply at Wolz. 'Frozen, of course.'

'Of course.'

'The weather is atrocious. There can be no guarantee. The U-boat simply needs a crew, you say? No supplies?'

'None that I am aware of.'

The phones, which had been ringing continuously, now all ceased, as though some gigantic muffler had clamped over them all. A gefreiter marched into the operations shack under guard, the escort extremely large and tough-looking men, smart, their weapons ready, their insignia gleaming. A senior N.C.O. led the prisoner and escort through the far door. The gefreiter looked green, ill, hopeless.

Wolz looked at the Hauptmann.

The Luftwaffe officer shook his head.

'The gefreiter? He's for it. He'll get the chop.'

And the Luftwaffe Hauptmann drew the edge of his palm swiftly across his neck.

'Kaput.'

Wolz did not enquire what the gefreiter had done. That seemed out of another world. He needed two transport aeroplanes to get his crew to Narvik. The obstacles seemed insuperable.

He must keep on trying. He had to.

Cousin Manfred. Cousin Manfred, the hell-raising, high-flying, gallant Luftwaffe pilot. How many times Manfred had boasted of his aeroplanes! Well, if the Luftwaffe did not deliver the goods now, the U-boat arm would suffer. The irony was not lost on Baldur Wolz.

'My orders have been approved by the Luftwaffe.' He spoke in a detached, crisp, General-Staff way, as though everything he said would automatically be accomplished. He could not despise himself for what he was now doing. Besides the absolute necessity of carrying out his orders, no thoughts of deception or trickery or self-contempt at chicanery could for one moment be allowed to influence him. A weaker personality might have experienced shame. Baldur Wolz, because he saw the way ahead, for this one time, very clearly, pressed on with only thoughts of what he must do to guide him.

So, in that harsh, arrogant tone, he said what he had to say.

'At H.Q. they will confirm your instructions. Two Ju52s. General Graf von Krugel is a personal friend. A telephone call will speedily set the matter straight ...'

The Hauptmann pushed his spectacles back again and sat up.

'General von Krugel? Of course. Of course.'

Wolz decided not to push any further. He could have gone on, and enlarged on von Krugel's expressed opinions that the Luftwaffe and the Kriegsmarine, particularly the U-boat arm, should work in close collaboration. The view was unusual. Göring was jealous of his Luftwaffe. Dönitz had often to whistle for aerial support. But Wolz felt a single nudge was sufficient.

'The aeroplanes?'

'I can find you two Tante Jus. We pride ourselves in the Geschwader that we are up to any emergency. But there is the difficulty of landing. That is out of the question for now.'

'The frozen lake? Hartvigvatn, you said?'

'That will not be ready for two days at the earliest. It seems, my dear Herr Oberleutnant, that much though we would like to assist you, we are unable through force of circumstances to do so.'

Wolz took out one of his black cheroots, snapping the silver case shut thoughtfully. He had to ration the cigars for the time being; but a long cool drag was called for now.

Baldur Wolz was not one of your deep-blue salt-water sailors pig-ignorant of aircraft, seeing in aeroplanes only buzzing interfering nuisances. He was well aware of range and load limitations. So now he lit his cigar and blew a thin streamer of smoke into the corner of the heated operations room.

'In that case, Herr Hauptmann, I must call on your co-operation and generosity once more. It will need three transports –'

'Three!'

'Yes. If we cannot land we must use another method of reaching our U-boat.'

CHAPTER EIGHT

Kurt Nolde finished up with his oily rag and looked with some pride and satisfaction and self-respect at his 1.3 centimetre MG 131. The machine gun would not let him down. His position in the dorsal cockpit of his Tante Ju could be one of critical importance. No! *Was* one of critical importance, should the big lumbering three-engined transport be attacked from the air.

The Norwegians were still fighting. They had an air force of relics from the past, to be sure; but Kurt Nolde was prepared to shoot Hurricanes and Spitfires out of the air if they flashed into his sights.

His thick fingers in the heavy gloves gripped the butt and his right forefinger curved around the trigger. Yes. He would much prefer to be back in his beloved Bavaria; but if he had to be anywhere now there was a war on, it was here, behind a machine gun, ready to shoot down any idiot fool enough to tangle with the Luftwaffe.

Sounds of men talking in loud, confident voices, covering apprehensions quite unfamiliar to Kurt Nolde, floated up from the slush-covered tarmac. He looked over the side. What a weird bunch these sailors were! They stood around the plane waiting. Patches of mist rolled past the end of the field and the light was poor. If they didn't get off soon they never would this day.

The sailors were U-boat men. Nolde gave a little grimace. The idea of being a sailor was bad enough. But the thought of going down into the cold dark sea, voluntarily slipping under the waves, created in him a revulsion he had no need to explain.

Give him the wide expanses of the sky every time!

'They may be made out of old scrubbing boards,' said a powerful, dark, hairy fellow in the Navy uniform, bundled up against the cold. 'But I'm told they do fly.'

'The wings have great slits in them,' observed a slimmer fellow, quick and alert. 'I don't care for that.'

'That's to ease the air-pressure so they won't fall off,' said another sailor, brash and confident.

Nolde scowled up in the dorsal turret. Time he went below and sorted these fellows out. The Luftwaffe was the pride of the German forces, and chaps who skulked about in steel coffins under the sea ought to realise that.

Looking over the corrugated aluminium fuselage again, Nolde saw the officer approaching. He looked a very devil, did this one. Big and yet not tall, tough and powerful and with a wicked black cheroot stuck up in the corner of his mouth, he strode along as though ready to strike with unexampled ferocity, to react to any situation with lightning reflexes. Nolde noticed how the men braced up when this Oberleutnant appeared.

Leutnant Cramer, the pilot, engaged the U-boat officer in conversation, waving his arms, appearing excited. Nolde had no need to be told what was going on. The tendrils of mist creeping past the edge of the field were clear evidence of what was the matter.

With a grunt, which said, more or less, that the Luftwaffe would decide if it was fit to fly or not, and it was not Nolde's decision but that of the pilot, the gunner ducked below.

If they took off for Narvik it would be a long cold haul.

He intended to find something warming to put into his belly before they took off. That was what a thoughtful man owed his own digestion and well-being.

'You are quite mad, Herr Oberleutnant. You understand that I speak in the utmost friendship. But if you insist on flying to Narvik it is essential we take off at once.'

'I may very well be mad, Herr Leutnant. Sometimes I think it is foolish these days not to be mad. And, yes, I do insist on flying to Narvik. And, no, we cannot take off just yet.'

'If you do not make up your mind very soon, we will not fly today.' Leutnant Cramer, a thin, tense man with the nervous gestures of an actor and a slender cigarette drooping from his mouth, waved a hand at the coiling mist.

'I understand.' Wolz glanced at his watch. 'Give me five minutes more.'

'You said that five minutes ago.'

'Another five minutes.'

Cramer blew smoke without removing the cigarette from his mouth and stamped his booted feet. He hunched his shoulders and clapped his gloved hands together.

'Very well. But if we do not take off then, I cannot promise to fly at all today. Narvik's weather will be a right bastard, you can be sure of that.'

Wolz stared in an icy rage towards the road. Where the devil was that fool Forstner? He swung back to Leutnant Meyer, Forstner's crony, and, he supposed, someone who might know what the idiot commander was up to.

'Herr Leutnant Meyer. Tell me again what the commander told you to say to me.'

'Only that he was delayed and would be here as soon as he could manage it, Herr Oberleutnant.'

Meyer looked most disquieted. He had not forgotten his display when the Norwegian jager had tried to ram U-45. For that matter, no one in the boat had forgotten. Meyer was now a man on trial in all their eyes.

'That's no good to me.' Wolz bashed his gloved hands together and, for the thousandth time, thought about finding a new pair. 'Our orders say we must go to Narvik. The Kapitänleutnant has given me strict orders to take the crew there at once. There must be no delay. The Norwegians will finish off U-55 if we do not hurry.' He glared at Meyer so that the young Leutnant flushed uncomfortably. 'I do not intend to help in the destruction of a U-boat.'

'No, Herr Oberleutnant.'

Baldur Wolz knew perfectly well why he was spelling all this out for the puppy Meyer. He was building up the background to the story he must tell if what he was so darkly dreaming of came to pass in actuality.

'Get the men aboard, Meyer. You will fly in aircraft three. Leutnant Ehrenberger will fly in number two. If he gets back in time, that is.'

'Very good!'

Meyer trotted off, thankful to have something to do that would take him away from the baleful eyes of the highly unpleasant First Officer. As he rounded the corrugated tail of the nearest Junkers a figure on a bicycle rode up the road, pedalling like fury. Ehrenberger forced the bike along and skidded to a halt with a spray of slush by Wolz. His face was fiery red and steam jetted from his mouth and nostrils as he breathed deeply.

'Beg to report, Herr Oberleutnant. No sign of the commander. He was not at Naval H.Q. and the attaché knew nothing.'

'Very good, Ehrenberger. Get aboard aircraft two.'

'Very good.'

The Second Officer took himself off. Wolz reflected that no doubt the good Ehrenberger was a trifle disconcerted at Wolz's reception of his news. To report a skipper absent and unable to be found at a crisis like this should have brought a stronger reaction. But Wolz merely took his cigar from his mouth, spat a shred of tobacco, and jammed the cigar back firmly between his teeth.

Damn the fool Forstner!

Four minutes gone and one to go.

Leutnant Cramer appeared, buckling up his helmet straps.

'All aboard, Herr Leutnant,' said Wolz. 'We fly now.'

'Another few minutes and I'd refuse.' Cramer took a dour look around, at the mist which hung in greasy coils over the end of the field, at the lowering sky. 'But weather tells me Narvik is usable, just. If it shuts in before we are there on our estimated time of arrival we'll have to bring you back.'

'We're going in, Cramer. Just you get us there.'

The three Ju52s had been positioned ready for take off, so that no taxiing was necessary and their engines had been running to keep warm. It needed only Wolz's final word to send the three aeroplanes down the runway for takeoff.

With his foot on the step of the big port-side loading door, he looked back down the road.

A car was lurching along in the slush, and Wolz fancied above the roar of the aero engines he could hear a thin and distant hooting. His face remained as grave and immobile as though he stood looking down on to the grave of his best friend. The car swerved and righted itself. A figure was leaning from the window and waving wildly.

Of course, in the time it would take for the car to reach the aircraft, for Forstner to leap out and scramble aboard, the mist would not grow appreciably thicker.

There was time for Wolz to wait for his commander.

The engines roared louder, as though Cramer was impatiently nudging him.

The car skidded and recovered and bore on towards the aircraft.

Wolz ducked through the door and the crewman closed it against the outside world. Word was passed without delay.

The Junkers started to taxi forward along the runway.

Wolz shouldered through the press of men sitting against the fuselage sides and peered through a port. He could just see the car racing out on to the end of the runway. Then it vanished past the corrugated tailplane.

He did not smile.

Forstner was back in that car, raving and cursing, no doubt, chasing the aeroplanes that were carrying off his officers and crew.

It was a moment to relish.

Wolz found a seat and sat back, well satisfied.

To hell with Kapitänleutnant Adolf Forstner!

The three Junkers Ju52s lifted from the runway and slid into the air, climbing, on course for Narvik.

From scattered makeshift bases on frozen lakes, all that was left of the two Norwegian Flying Services, the Army and the Navy, struggled as best they could against the might of the Luftwaffe. A wholesale scheme of reconstruction and re-organisation had been planned at long last by the Norwegian Parliament; but they had left it too late. The American Hawk aircraft rotted in their crates on the quays at Oslo. The old Fokker C V.D. and Høver M.F. 11 aeroplanes must soldier on still. The Italian Caproni Ca 310 had proved a severe disappointment. Ironically enough, the Norwegian Naval Flying Service operated six Heinkel He 115As, German aircraft, and they were to capture two more in the fighting – B models. Old aircraft, disastrous lack of material, improvised bases, all these things militated against Norwegian Air and gave to the Luftwaffe its usual expected margin of victory.

Baldur Wolz, even without Cousin Manfred's enthusiasm to instill the right ideas, was, like every other good German, perfectly confident of the Luftwaffe's ability to beat any airforce in the world.

So that when he looked through a window in the corrugated aluminium hide of the Ju52 and saw two black dots rapidly approaching against the overcast, he blinked and looked again. They had just left Vaernes airfield – and a fraught time that had been, too! – and were on the last leg to Narvik. Bardufoss, which was the airfield for Narvik, was out of the question. The frozen lake was a possibility. But these two ominous dots indicated that the Norwegians had no intention of allowing the three Ju52s to go another kilometre through Norway's cold air spaces.

Leutnant Loeffler peered through his window alongside Wolz. Wolz liked the comfort the big red-bearded Chief brought him, a comfort deriving from confidence in the Chief's wizardry with engines of all kinds, with all the intricacies of handling a U-boat. But now they were flying through thin air, and two aeroplanes were diving on them with chattering machine guns.

'Who are they?' demanded Loeffler, outraged.

'Norwegians – and they are not welcoming us as friends.'

'I can quite see that!'

The two planes banked hard around after the first pass. They appeared to have scored no hits on the lead aircraft, the Ju52 flown by Cramer. Wolz just hoped they had done no damage to the two kettehund in the following vic.

He saw the biplane wings, the straining engines, and for a desperate moment he fancied they were Gloster Gladiators. Then he let out a soundless whistle of relief. One was a Fokker and the other a Høver. They were two seat reconnaissance planes. He was forced to admire the courage of the crews. Had they been two English Gladiators, the interceptors would have made short work of the lumbering transports.

The attacking aircraft banked around against the dull overcast and came in gallantly once more. He could see the cherry-red twinkle of their machine guns. They were aimed for the lead Junkers. They straightened out. Their wings became thin lines. They looked all engine and guns as they each hurtled down.

Now the clamour of the answering machine gun fire from the Junkers shook the plane. Up there in the dorsal cockpit, Kurt Nolde hammered his MG 131, sending out a stream of 1.3 centimetre death.

The tracers curved through the air lazily. Wolz found he was automatically working out ranges and rates of change, as though operating a flak gun from a U-boat's wintergarden, and adding in the two hundred kilometres an hour speed of the old Tante Ju.

The rattle of Nolde's machine gun gave some comfort to the men cramped into the box-like fuselage. They tensed up as each burst told them the gunner had a target, and that the target also had a target – them.

One of the biplanes was painted a dark olive green. That would be the Army scheme of the Fokker. The Høver was silvery white of the Navy. But both had the vertical red and blue and white tail of Norway.

A line of bullets stitched across the end of the cabin, making the men jump. One instant they were listening to Nolde's gun; the next the crack-crack-crack of bullets punching through the corrugated aluminium skin shook them. One bullet struck a tubular steel fuselage member and screamed away, a deadly ricochet that barely missed Wolz and vanished outside through a palm's width hole.

'Now is the time for you to order "Flood!" Herr Oberleutnant. Let us dive and get out of this!' Loeffler's red beard bristled as he spoke. His little joke had the effect intended. The men near him laughed and passed it on.

Then Wolz was staring in horror at the bloody bundle that collapsed from the dorsal cockpit. Kurt Nolde wriggled around like a gaffed fish, the blood spouting from his chest. He tried to scream and only bright blood gurgled from his straining mouth.

The bullets had smashed his whole chest in, and broken out through his backbone. He writhed and then collapsed, a limp, redly-glistening horror.

Wolz looked up at the patch of sky and the upended machine gun.

He reached down and stripped off the gunner's helmet and goggles. He put them on. He was not thinking of each individual action; merely that he had to get his men through to Narvik and U-55.

He pulled off Nolde's thick gloves and wriggled his fingers into them. They were warm. He felt his way up to the cockpit, and gripped the butt of the gun. The slipstream tore at him icy, merciless, making him gasp. Up here he seemed to be hanging out over nothing, with the corrugated skin of the Judula thin and remote, a fragile object to uphold him in nothingness. The overcast pressed down. Below, there were lakes and mountains and snow. The whole scene was one of wild desolation.

Then the cracking whack of bullets past his head snapped him out of that foolish, half-petrified mood, and back into action.

The machine gun was brand new and of a newfangled design; but cocking it was automatic, and the sights came on and lined up. Wolz got his eye in. He saw the Fokker banking around for a fresh pass, the rear gunner still firing. The biplane's fuselage looked dark and purposeful. He lined up, allowed for deflection, triggered a quick burst. The Fokker turned, her wings thinned into two horizontal bars. The plane swooped down on him.

He fired and went on firing, praying the gun would not jam. Smoke whipped back. Now he could take full advantage of the senses he had cultivated in the air, gliding, going up with Manfred, even piloting the tethered Bachstelze from a U-boat. The machine gun shook and vibrated and spat lead.

He saw the tracers curving away and swung up and saw them going in between the biplane wings. He swung the gun and the Fokker sideslipped and was past and gone.

Everything had happened with nightmare speed.

Wolz had no real idea if he had hit the Norwegian or missed him hopelessly.

He stared around for the Høver and saw only empty sky and the two following Ju52s.

With dazzling speed, biplane wings flashed into view from the starboard bow, swerved over him. A line of bullet holes appeared miraculously in the Junkers' skin and then the Høver was gone. Wolz had time only to point the gun in the general direction of the Norwegian and trigger a despairing burst.

He turned his helmeted head against the slipstream, feeling the cold flaying his cheekbones. He could see no signs of the two enemy. They must be keeping well away from his lines of fire, in the blind spots.

He craned to look over and saw the Fokker belting up the port quarter, half-rolling to turn in like a darting fish to take a fly. He got the machine gun going and tried to bring the line of tracers and the line of Fokker's flight to coincide, swinging as he shot, swinging with the changing angles.

This time he saw a tiny flicker of smoke spurt from the Fokker's radial. The engine hiccoughed and belched smoke. He saw no flame. But the biplane swung away, losing height, going down, going down trailing a greasy coil of black smoke.

One gone.

Where the hell was the Høver?

For some moments Wolz continued to look around the lowering horizon, at the clouds, at the mountains, trying to pick out the silver-white shape of the Norwegian biplane.

He saw no sign of it.

Presently he realised that the attack must have been broken off.

He let out a sigh.

But hadn't they come through well! The poor gunner of this Judula was shot dead. But Loeffler bellowed up from below, his voice thin and attenuated, that all was well. Not one of the crew had been hit. Wolz felt the relief strong in him.

'I think it is high time,' he told Loeffler when he rejoined the crew in the fuselage, 'for the scientists to fit wings to a U-boat. We'd do all right!'

If the weather was to be foul, then there would be plenty of snow. So one evil would be cancelled by another turned to use. This was Wolz's plan, and simple-minded it must seem to the experienced Luftwaffe men.

The three Tante Jus roared on across the sky. Below them, the contorted mountains and fjords passed as though a manic giant had smashed booted feet down into mud and flour water. Clouds drifted wetly. The snow lay there, thick and, Wolz fervently hoped, soft.

Leutnant Cramer's nervous gestures were beginning to get on Wolz's own nerves.

'It is impossible for us to land here, Herr Oberleutnant. Now, Bardufoss – '

'Bardufoss is far too far away. And there was an attack by the British down in the south – Vaernes may be too hot for you when you get back – so why shouldn't they be attacking up here?'

Wolz shouted; but, he told himself, that was to overcome engine noise and not because he was angry. Through the windows the fjords were visible, dull sheets of water, leaden, ice-flecked, inhospitable. The black outlines of wrecked ships could be made out.

'There has been an action here, possibly a battle. They are destroyers down there, beached, burned out, wrecked. I must get my men down fast, and down here.'

Cramer pursed his lips.

'But you are sailors! You've never jumped before!'

'I have. My men may not have done so. Now's their chance to learn.'

Again Cramer shook his head in disbelief.

'We have the equipment. The Luftwaffe operations room co-operated with commendable alacrity, Herr Leutnant. Just position us and we'll jump.' And then Wolz added, darkly: 'And any man who doesn't jump is for the high jump. If you follow me.'

The men were kitting up. The parachutes were the usual standard type: the RZ 20. Wolz knew it and did not much care for it. Developed from the Italian Salvatore model, it had a modified Irvin harness fastening awkwardly and suspending the jumper by a ring just above the small of his back. You had to dangle and swim with arms and legs. You couldn't control the chute once you'd jumped.

He set about his task with a rugged indifference to any qualms his men might feel. He had to make them imagine this was just a quick and effective method of getting down because the Judulas couldn't land in the snow.

He had given his instructions, crisp and incisive, and now he just hoped the casualty rate would not be too punishingly high.

The knee pads and leg bandages aroused some comment.

'You won't need those in the snow,' said Wolz, bluffly confident. 'But wear them. Regulations.'

Regulations would control these men until they marched, singing, through the gates of hell.

Warmly muffled up, wearing the narrow-brimmed steel helmets the Luftwaffe had adapted for parachute use, they looked different. Somehow, as he looked at his crew, Wolz felt the alienness of what they were doing. What were honest U-boat men doing flying through the air and jumping out with parachutes? The bizarre note in all this had not affected him in the slightest until he looked along the rows of his men, in the vibrating fuselage of the Ju52, seeing their faces all turned questioningly towards him. They might question; that was to be expected. But, also, he saw in those tough German faces a trust in him that he knew he must always fight to merit.

He pushed the moment of weakness away.

His orders called for him to put U-55 back into commission. Kapitänleutnant Adolf Forstner, who should have been in command, was for some unaccountable reason not available.

Wolz repressed the delighted laugh. The reason was not unaccountable. The reason was supremely satisfying. Why, he'd just flown off and left the idiot Forstner yelling and racing desperately and futilely down the runway after him. That was precious. And, he trusted, he'd worked out all the answers for the inevitable enquiry. The truth was Forstner had no right to have gone sightseeing off to meet old pals, as Wolz guessed was the case.

Cramer took the plane up the fjord and over Narvik. The town looked a huddle of snow-covered roofs, with half-sunken ships in the harbour, a scene miserable and cold and aloof, with the crouching forms of the snow-mantled mountains lowering down all about. Up Rombaksfjord a plume of smoke lifted. Smoke drifted over the town below. The water looked greasy and grey, chipped with ice. No place to take a swim.

'Can you see the U-boat?' he demanded. His own annoyance that he could not spot the stranded boat had to be curtailed. It was up to the airman to spot things from his chosen element. But, all the same, a trained U-boat officer ought to be able to pick out the familiar shape of a boat...

'No sign. And I don't like the look of those clouds pouring down the mountains. They're like great rollers.'

'Find a nice smooth patch, Herr Leutnant. We'll drop there. It's hopeless to look for the boat in this.'

There was a boat in the harbour; but Wolz could just make her out and the men working on her. She was a Type IX. Probably a Type IXB, and so was not U-55.

Cramer pointed and Wolz followed the gloved finger.

In the contusion of mountain and fjords of Northern Norway, any area bigger than a pocket handkerchief that was flat was regarded as a wide meadow. The land went up and down, rarely ever level. But this patch of snow slanted only a little. Maybe it would do. What was under the snow was anybody's guess. Wolz nodded and clapped the pilot on the shoulder.

'There!'

Wings wide and black against the pallid sky, the three Junkers swung ponderously for the controlled run-in over the target DZ. Wolz allowed himself to wonder for just a moment how his men were feeling, how they would react, and if any of them would refuse to jump. It would be easy to blame them. The prospects down there were highly unpleasant. But this was war and they had their duty. That was what counted now.

The clouds rolled down the mountains. To Wolz it seemed they were trying to race the aircraft, trying to obliterate the snow-covered landscape below before the men could jump.

'Come on. Come on!' he said voicelessly.

Cramer was well aware of the situation. He was concerned over his fuel, concerned over the deteriorating weather, concerned lest any Norwegian or English fighters suddenly appeared. The loss of Kurt Nolde had affected the crew of his Tante Ju deeply.

Now the scrap of laughably level white lay ahead of the labouring engines. The Junkers bore on. A crewman opened the port door and the men stood up, shuffling, still pulling their straps, holding their breaths, feeling all the emotions a man must feel walking up to the scaffold.

The decision Wolz had to take was not easy; but in the end the commonsense solution seemed the best. He would jump first. Loeffler would jump last. He trusted the red-bearded Chief to boot out any laggards, and after the example of their First Lieutenant to spur them on, the men ought to jump without hesitation. The landing would be the time for a few broken legs and arms, if they were lucky – and a few broken necks if they were not.

He stepped up to the door and crouched, gripping the two vertical rails. He looked out. The ground seemed to be going past incredibly rapidly. Glimpses of snow and the flick and flutter of cloud told him there was no time to loose. As soon as he jumped, the men in the following kettehunde would jump, also. That was his instruction.

He took a breath. He gripped the rails and leaned forward.

Then, with a vicious thrust from his booted feet, Baldur Wolz launched himself into space.

CHAPTER NINE

The RZ 20 parachute pack ripped open as the static line tautened. The slipstream buffetted into the canopy, beginning to fill it as Wolz dropped away. The rigging lines reeled out, unfolding from the pack. Down he went, falling freely, arms outstretched as though diving. Now the moment was coming when –

The jerk as the more than half-filled canopy hauled him up when the lines reached their limit almost cut him in two. He gave a great yell and felt as though his body had been slammed into a door.

He swung wildly, gyrating, spinning. The world span about him. Noise burst in his head and lights exploded before his eyes.

Then, and only then, he was swinging freely, going down, feeling the shattering sensations gradually ebbing away.

Damned RZ 20! There had to be a better way of jumping with a parachute than this.

He looked up and as he swung his vision cleared the canopy. Lindner was out. The others were diving out one after the other like peas from a pod. The canopies opened one after the other as Cramer held the Judula on a straight and careful course. Wolz counted. Thirteen chutes opened. 'Thank God for that!'

He looked down, past his booted feet.

The scrap of almost-level ground looked tiny. He must be mad! No one was going to land on that mockingly small dot of snow. The mountain fell away beyond, and the rocky crags, snow-streaked, jagged menacingly above.

Now parachutes spilled from the two Iron Annies following Cramer. There was no time for Wolz to count past the first four or five. He had to get down in one piece. Suppose he smashed himself up now! What a savagely ironic commentary that would be on his actions so far!

He had no control of the chute. It would take him where it wanted. He fancied there was no wind to speak of. He went down, swinging, his arms and legs making futile swimming motions, trying to bring himself headed the way he was going. For most of the time he went crabwise, sideways on. But he managed to twitch himself around. When he hit he must roll forward and over. It was damned tricky and most messy. If only he could *control* the damned chute!

The ground flew up towards him.

To judge the distance was frantically impossible. He thought he was there and let his body go limp, ready to roll over, and then saw the ground was a good two hundred metres off.

And then he hit.

He was drenched in snow. A great gout of the white stuff flew up. He rolled forward and plunged over and over, the lines snared all about him, cutting in. Snow filled his eyes and mouth and ears. He snorted and blew and then he flummoxed upside down in a heap, the snow half-burying him, his legs kicking wildly.

He pulled himself out and instantly something hard and wet and angular smashed into him and down he went, bowled over by a man who was yelling blue bloody murder.

Wolz struggled to his feet, thigh deep in snow.

The snow, curse it though he might, was the one thing that could bring his men to land safely.

On a hard stony ground they'd have smashed themselves to pieces...

With a heave, Wolz brought to his feet the man who had smashed into him. It was Meixner, the 2 centimetre flak man.

'I'm glad you didn't have your flak around your neck, Meixner,' said Wolz.

And Meixner laughed. He managed to find a laugh.

Other men were staggering up in the snow. They looked like a band of half-demented snowmen, black and white, blowing snow from their faces, bashing snow from their clothes.

One man screamed and dangled a useless left arm.

Another man from Meyer's aircraft lay ominously still.

When Wolz reached him, he saw the ugly angle of head and body. So they'd had their broken neck, then...

It was Pfirmann, one of the machine-room men.

Sanitatsobermaat Reche was shouted for and came splashing through the snow to attend to Hahne's broken arm.

Ehrenberger appeared, looking winded and with a beautiful beginning to a black eye, caused when his own fist had hit him in the eye on the instant of rolling on landing.

'Any other casualties, Ehrenberger?'

'Nothing apart from a couple of sprains and a bruise or two – and a black eye.'

'It'll suit you, Herr Leutnant. A proud badge of combat.'

Ehrenberger stared at his First Officer. God knew what got into Baldur Wolz at times like these.

The three Junkers Ju52s roared overhead. The old Iron Annie, Judula, Tante Ju – yes, the corrugated wonder had done them proud. Wolz just hoped Cramer would make it safely back to Vaernes and Fornebu.

'Now,' Wolz said to Ehrenberger. 'We march down to the town and report to Commodore Bonte. And we march like German sailors – and like U-boat men!'

Commodore Bonte was not in Narvik for Wolz to report his crew in. Bonte had been blown sky high and to hell and gone when an English torpedo, fired from a destroyer, had exploded in the after magazine of his flagship, *Heidkamp*. The English had sailed in with five destroyers and had cut the ten German destroyers to pieces, sinking two and severely damaging three. One scrap of comfort was the fact that the English, sallying in for a second bite at the cherry, had been caught by five German destroyers sailing up from side fjords and had lost two of their number in the quick and bloody affray that followed.

Now Captain Bey of the Fourth Flotilla commanded the Naval forces in Narvik. The overall commander, General-Major Dietl, of the 3rd Mountain Division, was now a seriously worried man. It had been envisaged as an essential part of Operation Weserubung that the German ships must return immediately to their home ports and not loiter about the coasts of Norway to be snapped up by the Royal Navy.

The Royal Navy had struck at Narvik. The ammunition supply ship *Rauenfels* had been sunk in the fjord by the English destroyers, and one of the oil tankers had been sunk. So the situation in Narvik was close to desperate.

The Germans must hold out until the destroyers got away and reinforcements arrived.

'You, Herr Oberleutnant, must immediately salvage U-55 and get her to sea. I must trim the English wings. They have a six-inch cruiser out there, and there are bound to be battleships and battlecruisers lying out in the offing. There should be plenty of targets.'

'Yes, Herr Kapitän. I shall look forward to that.'

The worries on his shoulders, following an unsuccessful attempt to break out, made Bey pass over without noticing the hard manner of this ruffianly U-boat man.

Wolz saluted and retired, knowing what he had to do, and totally unsure if the job was humanly possible.

As he said to Loeffler, as they stood on the jetty looking at the wrecked and half-sunken ships in the harbour: 'U-55 is lying on the beach up towards Djupvik Bay.' They looked morosely at the destroyer *Roeder*, moored alongside the pier. Severely damaged in action with British destroyers smaller than herself, and with inferior guns, she was now tied up to be used as a blockship should the Royal Navy try again.

'Djupvik Bay?' said Loeffler. 'That's just past Ballangen fjord towards Hamnesholm.' He twisted the map they had been given. Ehrenberger held the other edge and the U-boat officers stared at the printed lines that represented their coming field of combat.

'The soundings are all over the place,' said the Second Officer.

'There is a chance the Norwegians will try to stop us. And if the English have landed troops...'

'We'll get her off. And we'll fight her, too,' said Wolz with such a firm conviction that the others all nodded, perfectly agreeing despite the enormous problems.

The chug-chug of an ancient engine announced the arrival of their transport. P.O. Lindner at the helm, an old Norwegian Skøyter puffed up. Commandeered, she would have to serve. With her thin tall deckhouse and bluff bows, she was designed for operation among the fjords. She stank of old fish. But she would serve.

The men of U-45, who were now the men of U-55, clambered aboard. Rather, as Wolz commented sourly to himself, the men who might be of U-55. He just had to get the boat ship-shape and off the beach and to sea. There were targets out there and his job was to sink them.

U-25, a Type IA, was operating further down the fjord and had already given warning of the English destroyers. The boat Wolz had spotted in the harbour had left. She was U-64. Wolz's U-55 would be needed. He intended to think of her as his boat. That way the kind of spirit he required in his crew would be transmitted down. He would show his men they now had their own boat again. They were not merely salvaging some old clapped-out heap to sail her back to the breaker's yards.

As he climbed aboard the foul-smelling Skøyter, he reflected that perhaps U-55 was really in a condition when the best thing for her was to be broken up.

He devoutly hoped that was not so, and refused to credit it. She had been fired on by the destroyers, and run aground, and most of her crew had been cut down then. Some had escaped and were holed out miserably along the beach awaiting some kind of decision. There were, so Wolz had been informed, at least six men and an officer, the Third Officer, a Leutnant z.S. Riepold. They'd have to fit in with the ex-crew of U-45. Wolz was in command. There'd be no nonsense over that. None at all. He had regularised the position with Bey, and had been given his orders.

So, for the moment, the odious Forstner was out of it completely.

The Skøyter chugged out of the harbour into the dropping clouds and the gathering darkness and Wolz felt the tiredness in him. He gave instructions for the men off watch to sleep and decided he had best get his head down while he had the chance. He would work this little craft as a U-boat for the short time of the voyage and make sure discipline was maintained. As a U-boat running on the surface. If he yelled: 'Flood!' now and the Skøyter slid beneath the icy water, that would nicely complement the Chief's desire to dive when they'd been under attack in the Ju52.

Just before he dropped off into a light doze, Wolz pondered the information given to him in Narvik. From intercepted English wireless transmissions the Germans had learned that the British intended to descend on Norway and retake the vital ports and airfields. A raid on Namsos was planned. Certainly, it seemed clear that Narvik would not be left out of it. General Dietl's men in Narvik were desperately short of fuel and ammunition. Aside from the loss of *Rauenfels*, Dietl's transport in *Alster* had been captured and *Barenfels* had still not arrived. So the destroyers were painfully pumping fuel two at a time. And, as though disasters had not heaped one on another enough, two of the precious German destroyers had run themselves aground. During manoeuvring procedures, *Zenker* and *Kollner* had beached. *Zenker*'s damaged screws would hold her down to a maximum speed of twenty knots; *Kollner* had done herself such injury that she was completely unseaworthy.

No wonder the extra bite another U-boat could give was so vitally necessary.

Wolz was abruptly brought up out of a beginning sleep by the distant smash of flak, the splintering crash of bombs, the faint whine of over-revved aircraft engines. He gripped the rail of the puffer and stared aft. Flames shot up over Narvik. The damned British were bombing the place! He wondered what the aeroplanes were and if they were doing any serious damage. All he could do was press on to the beached U-55, and hope no intrepid British airman spotted the boat and decided to drop a bomb on her for good luck.

The dull lower of the clouds, the scutter of snow, the greasy grey wash of the ice-flecked water past their bluff bows did little to reassure him. A biplane came winging down the fjord, low, her engine spitting and roaring intermittently.

Agonisingly, Wolz stared up.

She was a Swordfish. He knew about Swordfishes. One had caused him a nasty dunking and change of boat.

The old stringbag might be a laugh; she was an aircraft Wolz would always be wary of. The wide biplane wings flashed past overhead, and Wolz fancied she must come from a carrier steaming somewhere altogether too close for comfort. Now if he could get U-55 shipshape and find the carrier! Now that would make all this effort supremely worth while.

No signs of fire shone from aft.

Loeffler said: 'They must have missed.'

'Thank God,' said Wolz. Then he added: 'But conditions are pretty bad.'

'They'll give us the cover we need. If the English attack before we are ready...'

'We'll be ready.'

When later on they spotted a tiny dinghy tossing about uneasily near the shore and a light flashed cautiously, Wolz gave the order to port the helm and they chugged steadily in towards the snow-covered shore. Above them the mountains, almost lost in mist and drifting cloud, showed long white streaks of snow. The wind was still not too bad; but the cold was intense. The dinghy pulled a little way out and the light went into rapid morse. A German signaller, surely, was handling the lamp.

'Send back: "Come aboard", signaller,' said Wolz, speaking in his sure, calm, in-full-control-of-the-situation voice.

Presently the dinghy bumped alongside and eight bedraggled, cold and hungry men clambered aboard.

'Beg to report Leutnant zur See Riepold, Herr Oberleutnant!'

The muffled-up figure snapped a gloved hand to its cap, which was covered by a waterproof hood.

'Welcome aboard, Herr Leutnant. Now, where is the boat?'

Riepold half-turned and gestured into the mazy darkness.

'We found a bit of beach after we'd been hit. She's still here. But the engines are shot and –'

'Chief?'

Loeffler stepped forward, broad and bulky and confident.

Wolz made the introductions. Ehrenberger stepped up. Meyer hovered. Wolz stroked his chin. Well. He knew nothing of this Riepold; but it was almost inconceivable that he could be more useless than Forstner's crony, Meyer. Wait until he could get a better look at the leutnant, and then decide. Yes.

The Skøyter puffed along in the darkness, the snow whirling away, the water chingling with a cold harsh sound. The engine noise beat back from the mountains. Not a star was to be seen.

Riepold told them all he knew. The Norwegians had shot them down like flies as they'd left the boat. Only her thick pressure-hull had saved them from complete destruction, for the Norwegians had nothing heavier than light machine guns. A P.O. and six men had been saved beside himself, and they had a beastly time of it until they'd found the boat and reported in. Riepold looked dispirited. He seemed to think Wolz was wasting his time. Wolz ignored that. Riepold was by a couple of months senior to Meyer, so if he decided for the officer from U-55, as he felt he must, at least he would have legality on his side.

At least, Leutnant Riepold knew his business. He led the chugging Skøyter in directly towards the beached boat. Cautiously, Wolz ordered the engine stopped. Ehrenberger and Riepold, with an armed party, would go ashore and investigate. Wolz wanted to go himself; but protocol demanded otherwise. Thinking like a commanding officer was a knack he had already mastered; it was a matter of understanding this awful business of sending other men into danger and to possible death and of yourself watching them go.

He knew very well why he had chosen to keep the Chief with him in the same aircraft.

The cold bit, the snow drifted, the water lapped unpleasantly at the sides of the Skøyter. The landing party vanished in the darkness. Wolz gripped the rail and stared futilely at the shore, a black mass, cloud-wrapped, mysterious and hostile.

He had to wait. And waiting was the very devil.

He'd waited on that leave to go and visit Trudi von Hartstein. The odd mental resistance in his warped brain refused him personal permission just to walk over to the castle, or borrow a Mercedes, and see Trudi. But the chance meeting he hoped for did not happen, and it seemed all too clear to him that Trudi herself was not going to come over and see him.

Cousin Siegfried had said only one more word about the S.S. Sturmbannführer Wolz had so recklessly knocked about after the boor's sadistic attempt on Heidi, and that to the effect that the S.S. knew how to take care of their own. Wolz could read no threat into the words. Siegfried was tacitly telling him that the Sturmbannführer would not be avenged by his brother S.S. officers.

That nasty incident had occurred after the unsettling last meeting and parting with Trudi. He could still see her in the long nightdress, standing on the old stairs in the candlelight. He could still feel the smooth softness of her skin on his hands. How her hair had flowed and shone in the candlelight!

He hadn't seen Heidi much after that, and Lottie had preoccupied his time. But – but he must manufacture some excuse to see Trudi before he reported to the training base on the Baltic and a new U-boat. He must.

'I do not know who they were. I have not seen them before. They have not been to Castle Hartstein before today.'

Wolz did not like the sound of this.

He flicked Jupiter around and jogged away, at a loss, striking along the gravelled road instead of cutting up over the long hill towards the trees.

The breeze freshened a trifle. He knew very well why he rode this way. For all his let-down feeling, he rode here because this way was the way Trudi and her unknown friends would drive back to the castle.

He saw the lights of their car some way off, twin probing fingers flickering in and out of the trees and shrubs fringing the narrow road. He reined Jupiter off to one side and the Mercedes roared into view, hurtling along, the lights splashing brilliantly ahead, the engine roar fragmenting, rushing nearer and then fading with the Doppler effect into a throaty dwindling growl. They'd roared past without seeing him. He saw them. He saw the high polish on the black Mercedes. He saw the young man and the young girl in the open back, laughing, hair blowing, their arms about each other. The driver was smoking a cigarette, and laughing, and Trudi sat next to him in the front, laughing, her long fair hair streaming back in the slipstream. They made a picture Wolz would not forget...

He heard the machine-pistol fire spurting from the trees.

At first he was completely at a loss. In the quiet, peaceful countryside, with the birds wheeling as the shadows dropped, the trees going to sleep, the last pallid glimmers streaking the grasses, the stars beginning to shine out – what had MP 38 machine-pistol fire to do with this?

He hauled around to starboard on the reins, dug in the spurs, and sent Jupiter springing into a flat-out gallop back along the gravelled road.

The explosion when the car burst into flames shot lurid orange flares through the starkly silhouetted trees. The noise buffeted back. Jupiter shied up, and Wolz forced him down and on. He belted around a curve and there was the car, burning fiercely, plunged into the trees. A man ran crazily, screaming, on fire, his clothes and hair burning, a human torch. Long before Wolz reached him, he fell and writhed and then lay still, burning.

With the feeling of ice in him, Wolz searched. The couple in the back of the car had been thrown out and were dead, their arms still about each other. Bullet wounds showed on the dark suit, on the gay dress. He found Trudi in the ditch, unconscious, her dress partly burned away, black bruising on her face, her side ripped and oozing blood where a bullet had ploughed through her flesh. She had been thrown clear as the car swerved after the first burst, in the seat where she might escape: the driver and the rear-seat passengers had been doomed the moment the hidden assassin's finger pressed the trigger.

He carried her back to the grasses and put her down. No bones were broken. Her face, he could scarcely look at her face, pallid as always, but now parchment white, the eyelids curved and bruised-looking, the ripe mouth lax. She breathed evenly. He began to think she was not seriously hurt. The wound in her side, just below her breast, could be staunched, and he wadded a handkerchief there. It was a mere scratch, something a U-boat man would laugh off with the Sanitatsobermaat. But a wound along the soft flesh of a young girl, almost scoring into her breast, a vile wound from a machine-pistol – two worlds had met here in violent collision.

Quite clearly there was an explanation for this murderous attack. Wolz had no idea what it could be. Perhaps Trudi had no idea, as well. Perhaps those who knew were dead.

Curious, he said: 'Do you remember what happened?'

'No,' She said it quickly. Very quickly. 'No.'

He allowed the time to drift along as they rode towards the castle before he said. 'Do you think you have any enemies, Trudi? I mean, real enemies?'

'No. I do not think so. But Ritter and Eric, they might have.'

'Who were they? Had you known them long?'

'Not long. Monika knew them. They were policemen, I think. They did not talk about what they did.'

This modern Germany held many secrets. Baldur Wolz began to think he had an inkling of what had gone on here. There had been cases of Gestapo men being murdered in out-of-the-way spots. But he felt a vicious anger at the terrorists in involving innocent girls. And one of them dead. If they'd killed Trudi . . . This was the way the great enmities of the world were fed. At the moment Germany and Russia had signed a pact of friendship; but Wolz's friends were only partially veiled in their words when they considered the future, and the manifest destiny that awaited Germany in the East.

So he had taken Trudi home and she had refused to have her mother awoken and the doctor was summoned, and her side was pronounced clean and of no real danger. Bandaged, given a sedative, tucked up in bed, Trudi von Hartstein smiled sleepily as the doctor left. The old crone who served as chamber maid, personal maid, maidservant and Lord knew what else besides, clucked as she went out.

'And tell him not to be long. What the Baroness will say . . . '

'Hush, Karin, you old chatterbox! I shall be asleep in a moment, and then you may show the Herr Wolz out discreetly.'

She looked marvellous. Her golden hair lay upon the lace pillow like sun-kissed foam. Her face smiled, despite the bruising and the bandages over the scratches. She held out a hand, smiling sleepily.

'Five minutes,' said old Karin in her surly, privileged retainer tone, and Wolz nodded dutifully.

During his wait a fresh idea had occurred to him, and he wanted to get back to the schloss to ask questions. He fancied this might be a case of mistaken identity. That, at the least, would make some sense. If some other car had been expected to be on that lonely road, and the assassins had struck at the wrong target, as far as the involvement of Trudi went, the affair could be explained. But before he dashed off back to the schloss on Jupiter, he had to make sure Trudi was all right, to comfort her and reassure her.

'The doctor says there is nothing wrong. You'll be perfectly all right in a couple of days.'

'And then you will be gone again.'

He made a face. 'If my orders come through.'

'I hear rumours that things will move with the Spring.'

'Rumours? Who have you been talking to?'

'Oh, no one. Some of Monika's friends –'

She held his hand, her fingers pressing. 'I am glad you did come to see me, Baldur. I do not know – you were very bad – but I think, I hope –'

'I can never be bad with you, Trudi. If I am called away will you write?'

'Yes.' Her mouth drew down and he took her other hand, holding her fingers crushed in his.

'You must try to sleep now, Trudi. Tomorrow all will be different.'

'But tomorrow Monika will not come through the door, smoking one of her foul cigarettes, laughing, and telling me what we are going to do today.' The pain in her eyes distressed Wolz. 'She was a funny girl, her father had some shop or other in Berlin, and he left for Bonn, so she could be with me more easily. I wonder how he will take the news.'

'The police will –'

'Oh, yes. The police will see to everything.'

He stood up and released her hands. She was almost asleep, and he heard an impatient cough at the door. 'Karin wants me out, Trudi. Sleep well. Tomorrow –'

But her eyes closed and she was asleep.

Going out he said to Karin: 'Look after her well, old woman.'

Karin bristled, her nutcracker face outraged. 'I don't need some fine young sprig of the Herrenvolk teaching me how to look after my mistress.' And then she added meaningfully: 'If it had been me you'd seen last time, instead of that old dodderer Heinrich, you'd never have got a foot inside the door.'

So Wolz, suddenly stupid, suddenly filled with bravado, said: 'I doubt that, Karin. I doubt that.'

The doctor was waiting for him in the hall, holding his hat and bag in his hand, his face strangely gaunt in the candle light. He affected a bow tie, which immediately aroused Wolz's suspicions, and his general air indicated fatigue, apprehension and – and a weird glow of self-importance Wolz found disconcerting.

'She is asleep, doctor. Thank you for –'

'The accident was of no account. Horses will shy. I am surprised Fraulein Trudi was thrown.'

Wolz gaped.

'Horses? But the car –'

'No, Herr Wolz. There was no car. You were seen to ride in with the Fraulein Trudi on your horse. Clearly, she was thrown from her own. Perhaps she should not have been out riding so late, with a stranger.'

The painful rush of blood to his forehead made Wolz catch himself in time, and his instinctive reaction was not lost on the doctor. This was Herr Doktor Engel. A very old family friend, privy to much of the family history of the von Hartsteins. But when the man tried to tell Baldur Wolz that what had occurred had not occurred...

'You understand, Herr Wolz. The Fraulein Trudi fell from her horse. Nothing will be said of this in the village.'

Wolz thought he might be gaining a glimmering of light through the madness.

'But the car? The dead bodies? The gunfire?'

'No one knows what you are talking about. I assure you, in all seriousness, that you should take what I tell you to heart.' And then the Herr Doktor scraped up a smile. 'After all, your honour as a German officer demands that you protect the good name of a lady, yes?'

Wolz nodded. That went without saying, and the man was a boor to mention it. But he had reason. There was a very great deal more going on here than simple sailorman Wolz knew, that was painfully obvious.

'I shall make enquiries.'

'Carefully, carefully. This news is deadly. I do not warn you or threaten you, Herr Wolz. But your own life could be in danger if you do not keep silence.'

Again Wolz felt his temper flare. But, and again, he held himself in. He wanted no harm coming to Trudi. She'd been in enough trouble tonight, as it was...

Sarcasm, Wolz reflected, would not work with this doctor. There was about him that dedicated air that shrugged off sarcasm as a mere idiotic irritation, fit only for children.

Instead of being sarcastic, then, he said: 'And if I do keep silence, how can you guarantee the Fraulein Trudi will come to no harm, be safe?' Even as he added those last words he felt the strangeness of them, the oddness of this situation. Here, in the heart of Germany! The countryside around slept peacefully, the war was miles away, out across the grey seas. Here all should be, if not sweetness and light, then certainly not burned-out cars and machine-pistol gunfire and incinerated bodies.

Was this something of the New Germany, this brave Third Reich, that the odd-men-out at Academy had whispered of?

He bid a stilted farewell to Doctor Engel and rode off. When he passed the spot where the ambush had taken place, the gravelled road was freshly brushed. The remains of the car had gone. There was no sign of the bodies apart from a faint lingering taint on the air of charred flesh. He rode on, head bent, pondering.

Next day he asked a few seemingly casual questions, and his uncle answered as casually that nothing was known of strangers in the district, strangers in big official Mercedes. He went across to Castle Hartstein again, and was astounded, baffled, filled with fury to be told, somewhat offhandedly, by Heinreich the retainer, that the Fraulein, and her mother the Baroness Elizabeth, had gone to visit friends in Bonn. He could not see her. And the next day his orders had come and it was Kiel and U-45 and that confounded idiot Kapitänleutnant Adolf Forstner.

And that had led him directly here, up a Norwegian fjord, searching for a stranded U-boat in the snow and darkness.

A low-voiced hail floated across the greasy water.

Ehrenberger and Riepold and their party appeared in the dinghy. The snow cut more briskly and Wolz hunched into his leather coat. He did not attempt to light one of his precious cigars.

'All clear, Herr Oberleutnant.'

Ehrenberger handed himself over the gunwale. He looked frozen.

'At least, all clear as far as we could see.' He shook himself and bashed snow clear of his shoulders. 'It's thick and cold out there, Baldur. But we found her. She's capable of being got off.'

'Start the engine. Cox her in, please, Ehrenberger.

Riepold, get up into the bows and help guide us. You others stand clear.'

Ehrenberger's words had caused Wolz a breeze of alarm. The alarm was minor; but he felt it. He had felt it when Doctor Engel had warned him about Trudi. He felt the same itch now. Carefully, the Skøyter moved through the darkness, through the falling snow, through the ice-flecked water, towards the ominous darkness of the beach and a stranded U-boat.

Only when he could make out her outlines did Wolz give a soft order to stop engines. They glided on with only the chuckle of water to herald their arrival, like conspirators. Wolz eyed the loom of the mountains through the snow and darkness. They were there, fateful, leering down, holding the men and the boats below cupped in their trap.

The gunfire broke in a long stuttering burst that swept across the deck line like a scythe of blood.

Meixner let out a shriek and span about, his body contorted, his face a mask of blood. Other men screamed and fell. Wolz felt the pluck of bullets at his sleeve.

'They've got us boxed in!' he yelled. 'Make for the boat! Hurry! Hurry!'

The Skøyter bumped the saddle tanks. The bullets swept the deck and clanged form metal. In seconds they could all be very messily dead.

CHAPTER TEN

Directly before Wolz, a seaman grunted and doubled up. Wolz did not see who it was. He collided with the man, grabbed him in instinctive reaction, felt the wet stickiness. Bullets clanged madly from the conning tower. The hatch came up with a jerk. Men were tumbling on to the U-boat, yelling. The gunfire blattered unceasingly; yet in the confused darkness much of the effect went astray. The Skøyter was being cut to ribbons; after that first scything burst across the deck of the U-boat, the fired broomed away.

Wolz let out a stentorian bellow.

'Get below! On the double! Move!'

Men were stumbling and falling. A man screamed, spinning about, toppled into the water. If the bullets had not killed him the water would.

Meixner, the 2 centimetre flak expert, was dead. Wolz leaped up to the wintergarden. If the gun would not work, if there was no ready-use ammunition, if, if...

He grabbed the metal, feeling the cold strike through, chilling his gloved fingers.

The butt snugged up and he swung the long barrel, aiming at the distant pinpricks of fire from the snow-shrouded mountainside.

A dark bulk at his side turned out to be Meindl, a seaman with the broadest smile that could comfortably fit between his ears. He rattled the ammunition in a professional way and said, quite calmly: 'All ready to fire, Herr Oberleutnant.'

'Good man.'

Wolz let rip a long stuttering burst, spraying the distant dot of machine gun fire, trying to keep the gun centred and yet letting a few shells whip off in concentric patterns for good luck. The machine gun stopped firing at once. The men were pouring off the Skøyter and on to the U-boat. They were yelling and pushing; yet their discipline did not break down.

Wolz eased off the trigger. Those bastards out there would shoot again in a second; he counted four, carefully, and with the flak centred on the same bearing and angle let rip another sudden burst.

He just hoped that would smoke them out as they lifted their heads.

Most of the U-boat men were down the hatch now. Only a few more minutes. Then a machine gun bullet would never punch through the pressure hull, although he felt exceedingly uncomfortable about the saddle tanks.

The Chief appeared.

'The engines are shot to hell and gone, Baldur. But they can be fixed.'

Even then Wolz noted how Loeffler did not say: 'I can fix them.'

'How long?'

'Three hours, give or take fifteen minutes.'

'Then make it less, Chief. It'll be light soon.'

The Norwegian machine gun had remained silent. Just how many men were out there? They didn't believe the Germans came as friends. Wolz wondered if it would be worth taking a flanking party out and shooting them up from their own side. Perhaps, if the fire got too hot, it would be worth doing...

A rifle shot pranged off the rail of the wintergarden.

A few more rifle shots punched through the snow.

Wolz trained the flak around and let rip with a few controlled bursts. He had little hope of hitting anything; but if he could keep their heads down for long enough...

Ehrenberger appeared.

'All aboard, Herr Oberleutnant.'

'Very good. Volunteer gun crew to man the flak.'

'Very good.'

Meindl said: 'I can handle the flak, Herr Oberleutnant. Meixner talked well, poor devil.'

'Keep their heads down. And don't get shot.'

Wolz let Meindl take over the gun and clambered into the bridge. The smells of the U-boat came up strong and pungent; yet there was a mustiness about them, mixed with the cold and damp. He felt a surge of confidence. They'd have this U-55 shipshape and off the beach very soon. And then...

The volunteer flak party tumbled out. Ehrenberger, nonchalant, chivvied them along and then spoke to Wolz.

'The 10.5, skipper?'

Wolz noted the use of the word. He did not correct Ehrenberger. He luxuriated – as he had before, in other illicit circumstances – in the simple word, 'Skipper'.

'Yes. Volunteers. They can open up if the machine-gun fires again. Not otherwise. A trump card.'

'Very good!'

Wolz dropped down the ladder, ducked through into the control room. The dials and switches, the valves and wheels and levers, the smell and feel of it. This was like coming home.

He was pleased to see the men were at action stations, as though ready to dive or shut up for depth charging. There'd be some of that before long, too.

He went aft to the engine room.

Here the Chief was in his element. The harsh lighting looked pallid and wan. The batteries were almost gone.

'How's it coming, Chief?'

'If you want my opinion of the engines, skipper, I'll give it to you, gratis and for nothing. As to these engines in particular – ' An enormous spanner caught the light and flashed grease as Loeffler bent over the diesels. His powerful body bulked in the cramped confines. He knew what he was doing. 'Three hours. You'll have to keep those fellows off our necks that long.'

'They won't charge us with the flak to consider. And we'll serve them nastily before that. Just keep working, Chief.'

'Oh, surely. I'll keep working with my engine-room boys while you gallant lads aloft have all the fun.'

Refreshed, Wolz went back to the control room. The control room P.O. was carrying out a meticulous inspection. The next hour was spent in checking over the U-boat. All that they could check, they did. The boat had been run ashore with far less damage than the poor old U-45. U-55 could float and dive and fight still. If the men hadn't abandoned her and been cut down, they could have refloated her themselves. But the engines were a problem, a worry. The Chief just had to get them going, otherwise they'd be dead ducks.

When the time was ripe, Wolz gave orders for all movables to be transferred aft. The scene inside the U-boat's hull resembled some gargantuan market-day in a long narrow tunnel. Everything they could shift, they shifted, handing along through the watertight doors, the men cursing – although in the peculiar, tradition-bound U-boat way – as their knuckles were skinned and their shins barked. U-55 began to lighten forrard and sink aft. Wolz kept a sharp eye aloft as the light brightened. His men up there, relieved by volunteers at intervals, would have to be very carefully nursed. They would present prime targets as soon as the light improved enough for accurate shooting.

As for volunteers, they were not lacking.

After two hours and forty-one minutes had elapsed

since they had scrambled aboard in such haste, the Chief came forward to report. He smiled as he wiped his hands on an oily rag.

'They'll run, skipper. Of course, they may fall to pieces the instant you order both ahead full, but I think the string and sticking plaster will hold out.'

'Then get the batteries charged – and good work, Chief. We'd all have been sunk without you.'

Loeffler made a face, wiping his red beard, in which the oil glistened darkly.

'Just let's hope it won't be sinking with me,' and he went back aft again.

The diesels, which had been thumping every now and again as the Chief worked on them, now broke into full life. The needles crept across the faces of the dials. The batteries began to drink up the current. Wolz nodded. He went aloft and stuck his head out of the conning tower hatch into a pearly radiance that reflected, it seemed, from everywhere. The early morning mist dropped down, sending everything into grotesque monstrous phantasms. The mountains were quite invisible.

'Any sign of 'em, Ehrenberger?'

'Nothing, sir. Riepold suggested they might make an attack under cover of the mist.' Then Ehrenberger realised why Wolz had come on to the bridge at that time, and he ducked his head, acknowledging.

'I've a party below. We'll hear them, for we can't see them, that's for sure. I think we'll just have to shoot fast and make a lot of noise, make them think what foolishness they're up to. There'll be precious few targets.'

'If they get close enough for us to see them – they'll be on the casing.'

'True.'

What a crazy affair he was mixed up in this time! Wolz reflected that patching up a stranded U-boat, fighting off vengeful patriots who did not like this invasion of their native land, dealing with a sulky third officer – for Meyer sensed how Riepold would take over that position – and waiting for an anticipated English attack, were occupations far removed from sailing out and diving to sink tonnages. But that was the U-boat arm of the Kriegsmarine. They must turn their hand to anything in the U-boats.

Riepold bellowed up for permission to come on to the bridge, and Wolz gave a curt consent.

'I think she's lifting, Herr Oberleutnant. The last lot we shifted below made a difference.'

'That's good news. If we got stuck here – well, let's not think of that.'

As he finished speaking and the little silence fell, Wolz saw Ehrenberger open his mouth. He held up his hand and, fiercely, said in his cutting voice: 'Silence!'

They all heard the noise then. A scraping slide of pebbles. The noise came from the mist. It could be anywhere on a four point bearing. Wolz nodded down to the wintergarden.

'Open fire!'

The 2 centimetre burst into a scraping racket, the muzzle flash searing through the mist. The shots might be going anywhere; but Meindl had the gun under control. They couldn't hear the sinister scraping any more through the gun racket; but Wolz leant over the forward rail and shouted down to the 10.5 centimetre gun crew.

'Load with shell! Target – the mist over the starboard bow! Open fire!'

The gun crashed out with a splendid bang.

That should hold them for long enough...

Wolz flipped the voicepipe cover and bellowed.

'Full astern! Both engines!'

If they'd missed any serious leaks, any shot wounds, then they'd slide backwards into the fjord and sink. All the tank-blowing in the world wouldn't save them then.

The engines revved up with that superb coughing grumble of power that so thrilled a U-boat man. The fabric of the boat shook. They did not move.

Wolz looked over the side.

He could just make out the scummy grey-white water pouring forward past the saddle tanks. The screws were revolving freely, churning the water; but U-55 did not move. She remained fast stuck.

'Stop port!'

The roar of the engines changed as the port engine rumbled to a stop.

The boat rolled a little, twisting.

Riepold was looking nervously over the side. He'd said the boat was about ready to float free. He'd been wrong.

The gunfire broke for a moment and then began again. A few shots scuttered across the deck. Wolz felt the nervous strain, sudden, fierce, terrible. He wanted to order his men on deck, to run from port to starboard and back again. That way they might shift the stubborn boat. But he could not order his men on to the open deck, to run one way and another, with enemy bullets scything across! He couldn't do that.

He bent to the voicepipe.

'Torpedo room! Drain water from forrard tubes! Make it fast!' To the control room: 'Pump out forrard tanks, flood aft!'

The responses crackled up. The men below knew their lives depended on what the skipper did now. All his expertise was being called into question. And he was not even a proper U-boat commander, merely a First Lieutenant who had taken off without his commander.

The exhaust smoke hung greasily in the mist. The engine roared.

'Stop starboard. Full astern port.'

U-55 twisted sluggishly, trying to struggle free; but she still would not break from the icy grip of the rocks.

'Everyone with the exception of key personnel aft!'

The gunfire stopped from the U-boat as fresh ammunition came up. The men below would be ducking through the watertight doors, going aft. The machine-gun fire from the mountainside lashed out. Wolz could hear the sizzling slashing of the bullets punching into the water. If they got the range now...

Someone yelled. The mist coiled, drifting. Soon that would be gone, and their protection with it. The same voice lifted again and a machine pistol stammered.

Then – and the moment remained with Wolz as a moment of horror – dark forms loomed through the mist, appearing like monstrous ogres on the limits of vision, appearing and disappearing in the mist. They were trying to clamber up the saddle tanks. He pointed his MP38 over the bridge rail and let rip with a long angry burst.

'Grenades!'

Lindner was flinging grenades as though on the range. The vicious little explosions cracked through the din. Wolz thought he could hear men screaming.

A bullet spanged off the metal by his head. The periscope rang with the blow.

'The devils! I'll need the 'scope!'

The boat strained to free herself. Again he switched the engines, put the rudder over, felt all the tremble pulsating through the boat.

Leaning over, fists gripping the rail, he saw the gun crew at the 10.5 abruptly topple away, rag dolls tossed bloodily into the air, smashed to the deck. The blast of the grenade lashed at him. He gasped. When he got his breath back, he yelled: 'Clear that deck!'

His own machine pistol stuttered, cutting into the dark forms of men trying to run down the casing. They toppled away, falling into the water. He could feel the boat struggling and rocking. More men were approaching, and now he realised the mist was coiling away, lifting, revealing U-55 in all her stark nakedness. The Norwegians had timed their attack cleverly, to gain protection from the mist as they advanced and then, knowing the antics of these damned Norwegian fjords, to leap on the Germans out of the rising mist into visibility. Well, they'd a fight on their hands. Wolz wasn't giving up U-55.

'Leave the gun!' he screamed as Lindner started to rush the mounting with a volunteer crew to man the piece again. 'Your small arms! Hit them!'

Gunfire smoked about the decks. Gunfire lashed down from the mountainside. Gunfire ripped and tore into flesh and blood.

'Chief!' bellowed Wolz down the pipe. 'Both astern! Give me everything you've got! This is our last chance!'

CHAPTER ELEVEN

U-55 moved.

Like some obese whale, she slid grumpily backwards off the rocks.

The suddenness of it almost caught Wolz unawares.

Bullets spanged from the bridge and men were still savagely fighting on the deck.

But he bent to the voicepipe, his thoughts and emotions under control.

'Pump out aft! Flood forrard tubes! Men to action stations! *Move!*'

U-55 slid aft and down into the cold dark waters of the fjord. The pumping motors whined. The men took up their positions. Still the fighting went on on the deck.

'Clear that rabble away!' bellowed Wolz.

'Bridge personnel stand fast. Clear the decks!'

He saw the woollen-capped figure of a Norwegian lifting his arm to club down a wounded German sailor. With a quick riffle of carefully aimed shots, Wolz blew the Norwegian away. 'Get below!' The deck, which a moment before had resembled a slaughterhouse, now rapidly cleared as those Norwegians left aboard as the U-boat slid into the water leaped wildly for the rocks. The two parties broke and parted, one running and leaping forward, the other aft to the conning tower.

With a confusion of splashing water, of ice-chips spinning clear, of a great backward surging effort, the

U-boat plunged off the rocks into the clear cold waters of the fjord.

Only for a moment could doubts enter Wolz's head. He had given his orders; they had been obeyed. U-55 would not plunge on and down, like an arrow, straight for the bottom. But it was a moment fraught with peril; the slightest dereliction of duty, the slightest inattention, a simple mistake, and the U-boat would go on and down and carry all in her to their graves. Then Wolz smashed these fevered imaginings away. The boat ran out stern first into the fjord. Had she gone on and down they would have had to carry out crash-dive procedures. Had the boat been unmodified they'd have had to use the electric motors to go astern, and they might never have shifted her. The Chief had done marvellously well, and as Wolz gave brisk orders that would turn U-55 and bring her on course for deep water, he reflected that he had here the nucleus of a crew who could do great things on the war-lanes of the Atlantic.

The mist cleared off rapidly now, grey whirls and spirals like phantasmal maidens of the Rhine, drifting and swaying over the dark water. The light brightened. The course for home seemed set. Wolz had no business in Narvik, and his orders were clear. He had to take U-55 back for overhaul.

All the same, the English were due to attack, and Baldur Wolz was not one to let an opportunity like that slip by.

Here in Ofotfjord they were at the widest part and to starboard lay the smaller sidefjords – Skjomenfjord, Beisfjord, Rombaksfjord – with Herjangsfjord to the north-east. To port lay the Narrows, and the way to the open sea and Germany.

'Slow ahead both,' said Wolz. 'Steer two-seven-oh.' And to the bridge lookouts: 'Keep your eyes skinned for ships, now, as well as Norwegian soldiers.'

U-55 purred through the water.

Wolz itched to go below and check over everything thoroughly with the Chief; but he felt keenly that his duty lay here. He rubbed his bearded chin, and felt the tiredness in him, the way he felt dirty and unwashed. That would have to wait. The men could eat, for there were rations aboard. More seriously, there were only the four re-load eels left for the forward tubes, and one in the stern tube. He'd have one salvo and that would be that. They went slowly down the fjord, and Wolz did not hurry.

Then, with a snorting hiccough of great power and contempt both engines stopped dead.

Loeffler arrived on the bridge in short order, absolutely furious, his red beard bristling.

'The thing was made in Hades, that's for sure.' He went ranting on in his technical way, and Wolz, fully understanding, fully sympathised, also.

'Just do what you have to do, Chief. We're all right for a spell. If the English do come, we'll use the motors and do them no good. I don't want to dive until we have to.'

'Very sensible.' And the Chief slid below, muttering darkly what he would like to do to certain MAN diesel engineers.

With occasional surges of power from the electric motors, U-55 could be kept clear of the shore. Perforce, then, through the midday, Wolz and his crew waited. A sharp, a very sharp, lookout was maintained, with the lookouts changed every half hour.

He wondered how the refuelling was going, for the old converted whaleship *Jan Wellen* not only could supply the two destroyers at a time, they each required some 500 or 600 tons of fuel, and Wolz doubted if the impromptu tanker could handle that amount. The scheme would be to disperse the destroyers in the side fjords, and leap out on the unsuspecting British. That way, so he had been told, had secured the notable advantage for the Germans after they had been whipped further up the fjord.

Just after midday, a sighting astern was reported. This turned out to be the two German destroyers, *Kunne* and *Kollner*. *Kunne* was escorting *Kollner* down to Taarstad to act as outpost screen, for she was incapable of seagoing after her grounding.

Wolz took a hunk of bread and a sausage and ate them cold on the bridge. The sound of gunfire echoed along the fjord, and he stopped chewing for a moment, listening. Then, slowly, he masticated and swallowed.

'So the English are coming in,' he said, to no one in particular, and tried to wipe away the pleased smile. What lay ahead gave no real cause for gratification.

Kunne, firing from her aft guns, appeared at high speed running up the fjord, and *Kollner* limped to the south shore to lie in ambush in Djupvik Bay. The fire slackened and stopped. Wolz saw only a few shell splashes leap around the speeding destroyer, and estimated them as English 4.7 inch rounds.

Just after two bells in the afternoon watch, Wolz saw a Swordfish flying down the fjord. His instinctive reaction would have been far too late, for the plane appeared abruptly over the mountains, on top of them even before he would have had time to yell 'Flood!'

The Swordfish passed on down the fjord, and Wolz heaved a tremendous sigh of relief. He thought – but could not be sure – that her bomb racks gaped emptily. If the Stringbag had dropped her depth charges that could mean some other U-boat had been attacked and possibly sunk. Wolz felt the grimness of his thoughts.

Then, with U-55 still immobilised, he saw the snouts of two English destroyers appear around the point of Djupvik Bay.

He recognised them at once. Tribal class. Big, powerful, with eight 4.7 inch guns in twin mountings. They were gunships.

Even as they appeared, he saw the gun flashes, saw the torpedoes leap from the tubes amidships. Return fire came in from *Kollner*. But the Swordfish had reported the ambush, and the English were ready. *Kollner* got off one broadside and then the two English destroyers razed her gun deck. A torpedo blew her bows off. Wolz watched, fascinated. He heard the sudden gasp of awed surprise from the lookout and jerked his head up.

Even before he had focused his eyes down the fjord he heard the enormous slamming concussions. Tremendous explosions, ringing in monstrous echoes from the mountainsides, slammed up the fjord.

So before he could even see what was coming up the fjord, he knew. He knew the sound of 15 inch guns being fired.

He bent to the voicepipe.

'Chief? How are you coming? I have a British battleship up here I want to sink.'

The reply cheered him.

'You want a British battleship? I want a complete set of spares – '

The blamming of 15 inch guns blotted out everything.

'Clear the bridge,' said Wolz, still in that strange calm voice. 'Prepare to dive. Flood.'

As he went down the ladder and clanged the hatch shut, he reflected that it was not often given to a U-boat man to catch a tiger in a tight little trap like this. The battleship – she was *Warspite*, there was no mistaking that – could not turn easily. The fjord held her like a cork in a bottle. He'd got her and he'd have her. And spit out the pips.

The moment for elation had not yet come. But, if the Gods of War were with him, it would, it would.

All 27,500 tons of her, surging through the dark waters of the fjord, her 15 inch guns bellowing and shooting lurid tongues of orange flame through the murk, her steel plating grey in the greyness, on she came, H.M.S. *Warspite*. Her steering always suspect after her hammering at Jutland, nearly twenty-four years ago, where she had circled like a crazy loon in the midst of flame and destruction, she came on gingerly. Her attendant flock of destroyers ran and hunted ahead, and she crushed with massive power the game they flushed. The German destroyers might be much larger than the British, and have 5 inch guns instead of 4.7 – but H.M.S. *Warspite* was the trump card, a mighty capital ship risked so close to the enemy's airpower.

Staring fascinated through the periscope of U-55, Baldur Wolz did not lick his lips. He admired the great ship. He could see through the murk the massive citadel lifting between the funnel and the fore turrets. That was a legacy of her second refit, a major reconstruction undertaken in 1934–7. But Baldur Wolz knew that she was an old lady, a veteran of the earlier war, knew that her vitals would crush in under the hammer blows of his eels.

He read off the ranges and bearings and rates, the angles coming on nicely.

He checked through everything. He could see two destroyers flanking the big ship, and a little dint appeared between his eyebrows. They would turn instantly *Warspite* began to sink and venomously hunt down her attacker. Checking on, he saw that he would have just about water enough to manoeuvre; but the depths were shoaling. As they ran on, so the bottom lifted nearer and nearer U-55's keel. Presently Wolz had to face the facts.

There was ample water to float the destroyers; but the depth was quite insufficient for a U-boat to dive and escape to safety from the vengeful hunters seeking her life.

Warspite was on her way up to Narvik, and she would

sink anything German that floated on the dark waters of the fjords.

There was no question at all of not attacking, of allowing her to continue up so as to be in a safer place from which to attack her on her way down. The U-boat attack must be carried out immediately. The battleship would be gone, run past the best deflection shot in the world, in a few more minutes. She was coming up on to the sights nicely, now. That the U-boat attacking could not dive to escape, must seek to evade her pursuers in the mist and snow, could have no possible weight in the U-boat commander's decision.

No weight at all.

It just happened that the U-boat placed here to effect this attack was U-55, and the chance that U-55 was commanded by Oberleutnant zur See Baldur Wolz.

He thought of Lottie and Heidi, of Trudi . . . and as always pushed thoughts of Lisl away. It would have been nice to have seen them again. He thought of his men, fewer now, doubling up on duties, working like demons. There was Ehrenberger, with a fiancée somewhere in Bavaria. There was the Chief, Loeffler, with a girl in every port and most major cities in Germany. There was Lindner, just married, hoping against hope to get back quickly to Germany to his bride. There were the others, all with their own lives, their families, the reasons that kept them sane in an insane world – all of them must be subordinated to the demands of the service and of war.

It was said, truly, that: 'Who swears his oath on the Prussian flag has nothing left that he can call his own.'

The quartermaster broke in, across Wolz's sombre thoughts.

'The compass is not reading, Herr Oberleutnant –'

Wolz nodded. The Anschutz gyro-compass might very well give trouble up here; but the precipitous slopes of the fjord and the straightforward nature of the task ahead meant he would not need the compass. If they survived this attack – and Wolz considered that unlikely – then he'd worry about the gyro-compass. As it was, he did not think that was a worry that would concern him.

Warspite was crossing ahead nicely. A huge grey monster, sliding up the fjord, chasing German destroyers, possibly even changing the course of the campaign, she might destroy the German hold on Narvik and nullify the gains of Weserubung. Wolz felt he commanded a crew of dead men. The destroyers would be instantly on him in these confined waters. He could not dive. He could only hope to creep away in the mists and snow shadows under the cliffs.

'Prepare to loose!' came the calls, echoing up the pipes, clicking metallically over the phones, technical information, hard, precise voices, speaking professionally, not wasting a syllable, facts and unemotional figures, all coming together to form a single word – Death.

Wolz's eye felt enormously magnified. He stared through the periscope and saw the outside world, and all the rest of his crew waiting with him saw their familiar dials and instruments, the harsh white lighting, red-tinged for night vision; saw the bearded, sweating faces of their shipmates, and waited, knowing that their lives were in the hands of the commander. And their commander was preparing to throw those lives away.

Speaking firmly, without a tremor in his voice, harsh and matter of fact, Baldur Wolz gave the order that would bring Death.

'Loose!'

CHAPTER TWELVE

The old, familiar, exciting sensations of torpedoes shooting from their tubes thumped through the boat. Ram air hissed as the Chief compensated. Wolz stared through the periscope. Normally now would be the time to dive deep, to seek to evade, outrun, outguess the destroyers. Now, all he could do was creep along as close to the shore as he could, cursing this freakish stretch of shallows, hope to gain the normal deeper water in time.

As U-55 slid at periscope depth up the fjord, Wolz clung to the 'scope and watched with fascination the course of his torpedoes.

He had been through a very great deal to achieve this moment.

Useless now to recount the thorny path that had led here.

Training and more training, operational service, learning the hard facts of a U-boat man's life, finally a mad dash in aeroplanes and a crazy parachute drop and a desperate effort to put U-55 into shape – for this.

This!

Somehow, in that moment, as Baldur Wolz watched those carefully calculated torpedoes speeding through the water, their trail of bubbles clear but dwindling – or almost all of them – he could not summon up any emotion that would be recognisable to a civilised man.

One torpedo simply disappeared – probably it went

straight down and struck without exploding.

One torpedo veered off to port and went steaming off down the fjord.

One torpedo scuttered across the surface, sending up sheets of spray, barging along like a drunken dolphin, easily spotted by the English lookouts and avoided.

And one torpedo careered off to starboard up the fjord. But it did not go straight on up, as the one had gone straight on down, oh, no. This delightful eel circled. It swung through the degrees as Wolz watched, going through ninety, and then on and on, until it swung into one-eighty and completely reversed course.

Wolz said in his crispest voice: 'Hard astarboard! Full ahead port motor. Full astern starboard motor.'

The responses echoed up, and then the hydrophone operator, puzzled by the confusion of propeller noises, saying: 'Torpedo approaching, fast!'

'Yes,' said Wolz, thinking for an instant that, really, it was highly amusing. 'Yes. It was made in Germany.'

U-55 span like a top. She swung through the angles and her very own torpedo, which she had just loosed, raced back towards her. It was a race. It was a match to see if the torpedo could reach U-55 before she turned out of the way, and blow her sky-high instead of *Warspite*.

Still no words of complaint about the eels had passed Wolz's lips.

He had suffered from malfunctioning torpedoes on U-45's cruise. Now U-55 was experiencing the same trouble. Or, very possibly, it was a different snag. Up here magnetic pistols would be affected by the Earth's magnetism. Contact pistols ought to be better; but there was no guarantee of success even then for the depth-keeping mechanism was suspect – fifty per cent of the salvo; and the steering mechanism was obviously faulty – the other fifty per cent.

'Midships.'

'Midships.'

Now U-55 straightened up from her crazy sideways lurch. Wolz swung with the periscope standard. He watched the torpedo track as he snapped out: 'Half astern both motors.'

U-55 checked in her bull-like rush for the shore.

The trail of white passed down her saddle tank, so close that every mortal soul in the boat heard the whining thrash of the torpedo's propellers, like a monstrous buzz-saw ripping along their flank.

Wolz, the moment he lost the torpedo track below the periscope level of vision, swung the scope back to the cliffs. They were visible, snow-mantled, frowning, mist-shrouded and yet pearly with diffused light, all frosts and greys and coldnesses. U-55 would miss running ashore again, there was that to be thankful for, as well as not being hit by their very own torpedo.

'Stop motors.'

The periscope went up again and Wolz snapped off a quick yet all-embracing look at the English. Lord knew what they had been up to while U-55 had been trying to extricate herself from her own petard. Probably the English had been watching the German antics with incredulity, quite unable to believe what they saw.

What Wolz saw made him think the English had spotted nothing. *Warspite* was now well past. Two destroyers screening her on the starboard side were steaming on. The uproar had all been so fiercely and vividly visible from U-55, yet to the lookouts in their higher stations, steaming up the fjord on the watch for destroyers, the commotion in the water mixed with ice chips and the flurrying intermittent snow and the streamers of cloud pouring from the mountains must have passed unseen. Every time *Warspite* fired, some snow was dislodged from the nearby mountain slopes.

Wolz, prepared to breathe easy again, was just thinking through all the commotion what a magnificent sight

Warspite was, a still powerful and grand, if elderly, battleship steaming up with her 15-inch main armament firing, thrusting boldly into the lion's den, when U-55's runaway torpedo blew up against the cliffs with a deafening roar and an indescribably infuriating blast of flame.

Then, and only then, did Oberleutnant Baldur Wolz voice his considered opinion of the current German torpedo.

What he said was pointed, harsh, apt, and downright unkind to anyone in any way remotely connected with the manufacture, design, provision and profit-taking of the torpedo. He specifically exculpated maintenance and operational personnel. They were the poor fools who risked their necks to shoot off these miserable excuses for torpedoes.

An English destroyer turned like a wolfhound and sniffed down on to the suspicious explosion.

'Silent routine! Shut down for depth charging.'

The feeling in the boat abruptly tightened. Tension gripped them. Depth charging...

Every dial, every pipe, every tiny scratch in the metal about him, the way his cap sat on his head, the feel of his beard, the clinging dampness of his clothes, every trivial insignificant detail impressed itself vividly on Baldur Wolz in those moments of waiting.

He could see the small bow wave from the destroyer; she would not build too great a speed in confined waters. She would be searching for them now, listening, waiting for the peculiar sounds that would tell her hydrophone operators that they had located a U-boat. A drop of sweat ran past the corner of Wolz's eye and he did not attempt to flick it away.

The persicope came down under silent routine.

The noise of the destroyer's propellers approached, a metronome beat, a vroom-vroom, that sent shivers deep into every crewman. Everyone could hear what was going on outside their pressure hull. If the British depth charges came down close, even the pressure hull's tough Krupp high-tension steel would crumple. The sweat drop dropped. A tickle in his throat must be swallowed down. Those ears up there, they could hear a cough, so it was said...

Stuck up here unable to dive – and death bearing down on them.

The propeller beat approached. It was not exactly head on. They would not be run down, then, rammed and rolled over.

The destroyer's noises slackened and altered in tonal quality. She was turning. She was going away. Now – Wolz felt his stomach screwing up into a tight knot. He did not feel sick; but his mind was thronged with other times of intolerable stress when the depth charges had rained down and exploded close. Silence.

The propeller noises made that silence a beautiful thing.

'Up periscope.'

Wolz took a quick look. The destroyer was on a reciprocal course. She was steaming away. She had not spotted them.

'Resume normal routine.'

Wolz climbed down off the saddle seat and dropped into the control room. 'Herr Leutnant Ehrenberger. Take over the watch, please.' Wolz headed aft, for the engine room, for Chief Loeffler and for the last torpedo left in U-55.

'How long do we have, Baldur? *Warspite?* A tough old bird.'

'What the English intentions towards Narvik are, I don't know, of course. But General Dietl will make it hot for them. The Norwegians have so far, as far as we know, not been a major problem –'

Here Loeffler made a face, scratching his red beard,

and Wolz smiled. 'I'm talking in the grand strategical sense, my dear Loeffler, and not in the tactical as it applies to putting a U-boat into action. But my guess is the English will want their major units out at sea, as we do – did – and not bottled up. *Warspite* will be coming down the fjord and we must put this eel right before then.'

'I'll take its underpants off, and you can wipe its bottom and together we'll put the nappy back.' The Chief shook his head. 'But my guess is the thing won't work, still. There's something fundamentally wrong with our torpedoes.'

'I concur. But we must do everything we can. We can't just scuttle off back to Kiel with our tail between our legs.'

'Many a commander I know would do just that. And there'd be sense in it, too.'

'You mean I'm criminally reckless in hazarding the life of my crew, knowing the weapon I rely on may be useless?'

Loeffler went on methodically unscrewing the nut he was working on, and he did not look up. Wolz could not read anything into the Chief's tones as he said: 'Something like that.'

'That,' said Baldur Walz, 'is hardly the way to win wars.'

Now the Chief looked up. His face showed a hardness Wolz had scarcely marked before.

'Nor is risking valuable U-boats for nothing.'

Wolz repressed the insane rush of anger that filled him. He decided he must keep this on a light, personal level, for the moment condescending, if that was not too ugly a word, to forget he was *ipso facto* the captain of the boat. He relied on Loeffler as any commander must rely on his Chief; but in Loeffler's case he sensed a deeper agreement to Wolz's taking on of the mantle of commander, and he had no wish to tear down that kind of vital relationship.

'I know exactly what you mean, Chief. It is something that cannot be lightly glossed. But our job is to sink English ships, good weapons or bad weapons. I managed to fix up some eels which worked in U-45. I'm sure we can do the same for this one.' He hesitated, and added: 'Well, I'm hopeful.'

'I know it is our duty. And I do not shirk that. All I question is the risk to the men's lives and to the boat when the outcome is so much in question. If we sank *Warspite*, and I was killed, I suppose I'd manage to live and bear it.'

At Wolz's half-smile Loeffler, too, smiled. 'You know quite well what I mean. But if the damned eel misfires or goes off course again, and then we're sunk – I tell you, Baldur, I would be raging mad.'

Wolz bent again to the torpedo, his every action and word eloquent of the commander in command.

'We'll make this thing work and we'll attack. If it fails again we will have done our duty. No one can ask more of us than that. But if we turn tail now, I think – I could be wrong – that we would be condemned in our own eyes even if B.d.U. were to understand and pardon us. D'you see?'

'Oh, I see all right. I just think it's so damned unfair.'

'Of course it's unfair. Since when did you expect fairness in life, particularly in the middle of a war?'

Loeffler banged his spanner about; but he was forced to agree. The commander in action commanding bit, a role which Wolz, with the arrogance of youth, considered fitted him admirably, had worked in this low key approach. But Wolz was perfectly prepared to yell at the Chief and tell him what was to be done, and insist on seeing it done. He was feeling his way forward. He felt he had done the right thing here; but he could so easily be wrong. He pushed that from him. He must concentrate on putting every single thing right that could be put right with this eel, and then of attacking and this time of trusting the torpedo would behave properly.

In truth, he could see no other way ahead.

Of course life was unfair.

Life had been viciously unfair in getting his father so stupidly killed, rammed and sunk in his U-boat, right at the end of the last war. Life had been unfair in so quickly claiming his mother. Life had been unfair that it was not he, Baldur Wolz, who would inherit the fine schloss of Uncle Siegfried, and the lands and money and good things that went with it, but his Cousin Siegfried. Life was unfair in little ways, too, ways which could be pointed at as prime examples.

He considered it no small thing that life was so unfair to him that every time he was in the company of Cousin Lisl he became a bumpkin, all knees and elbows, sweating, unable to get out a simple sentence without stumbling and stuttering.

Cousin Lisl was simply wonderful, adorable, magnificent, removed from Wolz's orbit – although he railed at himself for his own stupidity – and she would end up marrying a high-born noble, a Junker, or given that this was the Third Reich, a very high official indeed of the Party. She had been born for fame, or so it seemed to Wolz. She had been sent away to a very good school, and he saw her only in holiday time, or when some great catastrophe – like the funeral of Great Aunt Claudia – brought the family together. Towards him, she was always reserved, not so much as withdrawn. They had played together as children, of course; but that was before she had become a young lady.

Beside Lisl even Trudi paled. But Trudi was the girl he had thought he would already have proposed to by now. If she would have him or not, he did not know. His prospects were only those of a well-connected young naval officer. Given talent, the knack of getting the job done, more good connections, and a very large slice of luck, he could one day hoist his flag.

Of course, and equally, if she married him, Trudi could become a widow very soon.

Every now and again he received a polite, stilted letter from Lisl. She would enquire after his health, trust he was keeping fit, hoped he was seeing something of the world, tell him a few tiny fragments of her life – tantalising glimpses into a way of life as distant as the Moon – and end by wishing him all good luck. She always appended a few scribbled words that said, in ink on paper, that she was looking forward to seeing him again. But, in his own hermit-like rejection of all good hope where Lisl was concerned, he would understand at once that these words were merely a polite formula, a perfunctory rote final salutation. He could gain not a crumb of comfort from anything or any part of his relationship – or non-relationship – with Lisl, apart from the fact that he had been allowed in this life to know her for a space. He was that far gone.

So he would think of Marlene or Lottie or Heidi, and reflect that it was time he tumbled Marlene, or his cousins would think he had lost the flair.

Truth was, he did not much care for Marlene, for the way she flaunted her half-nakedness, dressed up in black leather and red, black and white swastika armbands, with black leather straps, and a holstered Walther automatic. Her S.S. officer's cap would be pushed sideways at a jaunty angle that merely made Wolz see more clearly the meretricious nature of the costume.

She had taken to adding a smoking cigarette to her act, and whilst it was undeniably clever, and gave some indication of the strength of her muscles and thus of potential enjoyment, it still had no real power to move Wolz.

Cousin Siegfried, splendid in his S.S.-Sturmbannführer's uniform, stepping into the black Mercedes with the flags and the white-wall tyres and the ramrod-backed chauffeur and bodyguard cradling an MP38, had halted, his foot on the running board. The S.S.-Oberführer for whom Siegfried was currently acting as Brigade Intelligence Officer, with the chance of promotion in the offing to a position on the S.S.-Gruppenführer's staff, sat back in the car as Siegfried halted. Siegfried had time to whisper, quickly: 'It is a confounded nuisance I'm being dragged away, Baldur. You'll have to take the car to the station and meet Marlene.'

Then the Oberführer grunted words to the effect that the S.S. could scarcely wait until an Intelligence Sturmbannführer carried on a long private conversation.

Siegfried whipped around and flopped into the back seat.

'Very good!' he bellowed, and the car started with a smooth rush of power, the two motorcyclists roaring out ahead.

With this unexpected disappearance of Siegfried, the evening's entertainment at the schloss had been postponed, and Wolz, fretting at being posted to a new U-boat, was in half a mind not to bother to go to the station. But that would be bad manners, if not an indication of lack of breeding, and so he took the car and picked Marlene up. She categorically refused to return to Berlin straightaway, and insisted on going to the schloss.

'After all,' as she said, '*someone* will be there.'

In the event a mere handful of people turned up for the entertainment, Siegfried failed to notify them in time that he was unable to host them. As usual, Uncle Siegfried had taken himself off, only this time not to

Berlin but to the Ruhr, where he was to have a long series of discussions with the people at Krupps.

Helmut and Manfred were not at home, and yet Wolz was in no mood to act the host. He forced himself to appear genial, and even subjected himself to the torture of standing between an S.S.-Standartenführer and a Gestapo man of indeterminate rank and status, yet who commanded immediate obedience from his entourage and others who seemed to know more than Wolz did, and listening to a long disjointed conversation about the possibilities of the war.

Wolz wondered if he ought, because of the presence of the Gestapo, call off Marlene's performance. He went to the small room she had been given as a dressing room off the end of the long hall, and she pouted and flashed her eyes at him, whilst drawing on a long black silk stocking.

'Oh, Baldur! You are a droll! Willi Bockmann only came here because I told him where I was going. He doesn't want to be reminded that he is a policeman tonight. Now run along.' She looked up from her bent-over stance, both hands to the black silk stocking, her head cocked. Wolz suddenly saw how white her flesh looked against the black silk. 'But you'll come and see I'm all right tonight, won't you? As Siegfried is not here?'

He nodded, stiffly. 'If you like.'

'It's not if I like!' she flared at him. 'I think it's you who'd like it!'

He went out, saying simply that he would make sure she was all right later on in the evening. He managed to slip away from her entertainment and then went through one of the spells of crisis in which he manufactured excuses to go across to see Trudi and eventually found an excuse not to go. So he went into the library and found an English book – it was an H. G. Wells he had read many times, *The War of the Worlds* –

and kept out of the way. The time slipped by and the revellers passed out in their genteel or swinish ways, and he suddenly realised he ought to go and see Marlene. He did not relish the visit.

He went up the stairs and knocked on her door.

'Who is it? Baldur?'

So she was superbly confident, then!

'Yes.'

The door opened slowly, centimetre by centimetre, and a white, set face showed as Marlene looked out. When she saw it really was Baldur Wolz she threw the door back and motioned him inside. As he went in he considered the whole charade fifth rate, not worthy of the sleaziest Berlin fleapit.

But she surprised him.

She still wore her outrageous S.S. rigout with the black straps pressing her breasts, and the swastika flaunting on its chain between them. Wolz saw the dark shadows, the way she moved, the erratic motions of her arms. Her hair looked lacklustre. So maybe he would not be importuned, as he had feared.

'Have a drink, Baldur. God! I live on drink these days.'

He helped himself to a schnapps and stood, the small glass in his hand, eyeing her. He said: 'You look down, Marlene.'

'I feel down. Fancy Siegfried going off and leaving me. He knew I was coming here, especially for him, and that fat pig Gurke at the theatre keeps pestering me and I thought I'd get away – I'll lose my job if this goes on.'

'Surely any theatre would jump at the chance . . . '

'Don't you believe it, sonny. I don't leap into bed with the first man who whistles.' She drank off her glass and immediately refilled it, ignoring Wolz's instinctive move to assist her. 'I pour my own drinks.'

'Well,' he said, brightly, 'I just wanted to make sure you were all right. You have everything you need?'

As soon as he spoke he realised how she might take the simple polite formula.

'Everything I need?' She threw her arms wide. She really had a superb figure. 'I was blessed or cursed with this body. But what I need? I need – oh, it's not your business, Baldur.'

'No.'

She walked a little unsteadily to the chaise longue and slumped down, spilling some drink. It splashed on to her chest. She looked down. The schnapps ran down between her breasts, past the dangling swastika, down between the two supple curves Wolz had often contemplated on a dark night on the bridge of a U-boat smashing into the North Atlantic.

'Baldur!' She spoke a little thickly. 'Come here.'

He walked across, stood before her. She tilted her head up in the lights, staring at him. Her red lips parted.

'Kiss it off, Baldur. Lick it off. It's good schnapps and it would be a crime to waste it.'

Well, now...

He pulled out a handkerchief. 'Here.'

'You cold-blooded devil!'

She threw the handkerchief at him, wadded into a ball. He caught it. She let the schnapps run down her belly, past her navel, tangle in her hair. The liquid gleamed in a long streak in the lights.

'You know, Baldur. One day I think I will finish it all. I've thought about it, often and often. I will. I've plenty of pills. Old Doctor Rosenzweig gives me plenty of pills. And he gives me other things, too, to pay for the pills.' And she threw her head back against her outstretched arms, and laughed. The laugh rang wildly in the bedroom. Wolz wished Siegfried was here.

Leaning back like that, she deliberately crossed one black silk-clad leg over the other. Her high-heeled shoes gleamed their glossy black. She stared at him through half-lowered lids. It was all very fetching, and Wolz was once again his own man.

'Well, Baldur? Aren't you going to? Don't you want me?'

'I just looked in. If you have everything I'll be off. Big day tomorrow.'

She sat up, her legs snapped straight, her breasts surged as she took a breath.

'What's the matter with you?'

He couldn't be too cruel to her. Anyway, she was in some kind of trouble, and Siegfried would have to be told and help her.

'I'm worn out, Marlene. Really. I think I'll go straight to bed and sleep for a fortnight.'

'And the big day tomorrow?'

He smiled. 'That can wait – although I shouldn't say it.' He went to the door. She saw that he meant what he said. 'You turn in now, Marlene. You'll feel better in the morning. Good-night.'

She tore off one black polished shoe and threw it. Wolz heard it thump against the closing door, and he laughed. He had not behaved like a gentleman; but, then, he didn't believe in their ethics at all times.

So here he was, sweating over a torpedo that was probably a rogue, a dud, or simply a useless hunk of metal, and sweating, too, on the return of a mighty British battleship he wanted to sink. The connections were obvious. He passionately hoped that later on today he would not be calling *Warspite* Marlene.

Those two scenes with Marlene – they were miles apart, really, although they might on the surface appear to be the same. She was in some trouble. He had some interest, a little, not much; but he felt for her as another human being who was suffering. Her talk about killing herself could be serious. Anyway, he'd written guardedly to Siegfried, and his S.S. cousin could take it on from there.

Loeffler stood up and wiped his hands, looking thoughtfully at the torpedo.

'Everything is perfect. Now, if the thing does not work then it is the fault of outside influences. We can do no more.'

'Right. You'd better get some coffee.'

And Wolz took himself off to the bridge.

He gave the necessary orders and noted with a tightening of the lips the way the men responded. They knew they had all just been through a harrowing experience. Now their new skipper was taking them up the fjord, straight up to Narvik, to make another attempt, to have another crack at the British battleship. The feelings of the men could not be allowed to influence Wolz. With the engines repaired, a single ramaining torpedo that might or might not work, he went back up to Narvik.

Evidence of the terrible toll of destruction wrought by the 15 inch guns of *Warspite* lay on either hand. Blackened and burned out German destroyers, half-sunk, littered the fjords. Wolz looked at them as the boat went up the fjord, and the ice in him grew and clustered. This was the kind of result sea-power brought.

Twice more the engines broke down and were patched together. Loeffler shook his head, promising dire retribution to men who so wantonly abused good machinery, quite forgetting his remarks about the self-same machinery earlier. The fjord opened out and there lay Narvik, sullen, half-seen, smoking. And, at the mouth of Rombaksfjord, the huge sentinel-form of *Warspite*!

British destroyers were busy, and Wolz was cheered to observe evidence of damage to the ships. The British had not had it all their own way, then.

He manoeuvred carefully. This was a once-for-all shot.

The stern tube would give him the opportunity to go full speed ahead in order to escape the inevitable hunt.

That, at least, was one blessing. He read off the angles and bearings, estimating ranges, this time more judging the moment of release by eye and feel, not altogether trusting the marvellous mechanical and electrical bag of tricks that was the attack table. It was clever and precise; but Wolz was developing a feeling for shooting by eye and sense.

The 'scope came around. The sights lined up. Everything looked weird, uncanny, out there. The cold could be felt. *Warspite* towered against the snow flurries. Wolz bent to the eyepiece. This time they had to hit!

A tremor shook the boat and the 'scope vibrated.

'Hold her steady!' bellowed Wolz.

'The motors –' the Chief didn't say any more; but the tremors eased. But, all the same, there was an uncomfortable difference in the note of the motors, as though one was running out of phase. The sights came on, came on...

'*Loose!*'

The torpedo was running.

'Full ahead both!'

Let them get away, now, before the destroyers reacted.

They had done their duty, more than their duty. They were under orders to sail for Germany; but no one was going to deny that a British battleship was good and sufficent reason for disobeying orders. Wolz stared hungrily at the torpedo track. Just let the eel hit! Just let her explode!

He waited for almost too long and then ordered down periscope.

The stopwatches were consulted. The time ran on. The men counted. Tension, strain, a fearful withdrawal from the expected counterattack gripped them, made them tremble and sweat, and yet made them brace up, for the attack had not yet started.

The time ticked on.

'Torpedo running!' intoned the hydrophone operator.

What was going on up there? There was no report of destroyer screws. Wolz had to see.

'Up periscope!'

He looked, a quick searching stare. *Warspite* still floated at the head of Rombaksfjord. The destroyers were still busy – one Tribal had her bows blown clean off. But there was no sign of what Wolz hungered to see. The battleship floated serenely, and for all she knew or cared U-55 might as well not exist.

No reports. Nothing more. A big fat round zero.

The eel had failed them.

Wolz gave the course. Down the fjord to the sea.

He felt deflated, let down, absolutely dejected, like a knackered horse.

'I'll put in a report,' he said to the Chief. 'I'll put in a report that will sizzle their ears! They're sending us out to risk our lives with weapons with no teeth. By God! B.d.U. haven't heard the last of this. I'll make them sweat!'

The atmosphere in the boat would have done credit to the funeral of a Kaiser. The men crept about, keeping out of the skipper's eye. Murder hung in the air. But, gradually, as U-55 slid down the fjord, with the Chief nursing the engines and motors, a more sanguine appreciation gradually took hold.

'This fiasco will at least mean something must be done. We can't be the only boat whose torpedoes are useless. No, Chief. By the time we're given a new outfit of eels, they'll work. And then we'll sink tonnages! We'll make the English sorry they got into this war, battleships or no damn battleships.'

'We have to get home first.'

'We'll get home! We'll get home safely and we'll sail all the way to Kiel. We'll have a refit and then –'

'And Kapitänleutnant Adolf Forstner?'

Wolz had completely forgotten that fool. Now he was brought up short.

He forced a laugh. 'I'll worry about that when the time comes. Anyway, even he couldn't have sunk *Warspite* with eels with no teeth!'

Yes, Baldur Wolz would sail home and sort out his next boat. And he'd see Lottie and Heidi – and perhaps Marlene. He'd find out about Trudi and see if he could discover the mystery there. Would he ask her to marry him now? He didn't know.

What he did know, with a passionate belief, was that he would go on sailing in U-boats, he would continue to be a U-boat man. That, at the least, was assured.

ADVENTURE FOR MEN

THE SURVIVALIST #1: TOTAL WAR (768, $2.25)
by Jerry Ahern
The first in the shocking series that follows the unrelenting search of ex-CIA covert operations officer John Thomas Rourke to locate his missing family—after the button is pressed, the missiles launched and the multi-megaton bombs unleashed . . .

THEY CALL ME THE MERCENARY: THE KILLER GENESIS
by Axel Kilgore (678, $2.25)
Hank Frost is blood-hunting his way through the jungles of Central Africa. And he's carrying his best equipment, along with a vicious vendetta—against a crazy rogue commander who massacred Frost's outfit to the very last man!

THEY CALL ME THE MERCENARY #2: THE SLAUGHTER RUN
by Axel Kilgore (719, $2.25)
Assassination in the Alps . . . Terrorism in the jungle . . . Deception in Washington. And Hank Frost is caught in the middle—with a nymphomaniac wife of a general by his side who'll have him as a lover . . . or have him dead.

**THEY CALL ME THE MERCENARY #3:
FOURTH REICH DEATH SQUAD** (753, $2.25)
by Axel Kilgore
After losing his prize charge to terrorist kidnappers, Hank has to gut his way through a sado-masochistic torture team, neo-Nazi gunmen and a vastly powerful Fourth Reich conspiracy to get him back. He finds help from a beautiful Mossad agent who's on his side—so she claims . . .

Available wherever paperbacks are sold, or order direct from the Publisher. Send cover price plus 50¢ per copy for mailing and handling to Zebra Books, 475 Park Avenue South, New York, N.Y. 10016. DO NOT SEND CASH.

THE GUNN SERIES BY JORY SHERMAN

GUNN #1: DAWN OF REVENGE (590, $1.95)
Accused of killing his wife, William Gunnison changes his name to Gunn and begins his fight for revenge. He'll kill, maim, turn the west blood red—until he finds the men who murdered his wife.

GUNN #2: MEXICAN SHOWDOWN (628, $1.95)
When Gunn rode into the town of Cuchillo, he didn't know the rules. But when he walked into Paula's cantina he knew he'd learn them. And he had to learn fast—to catch a ruthless killer who'd murdered a family in cold blood!

GUNN #3: DEATH'S HEAD TRAIL (648, $1.95)
When Gunn stops off in Bannack City, he finds plenty of gold, girls and a gunslingin' outlaw. With his hands on his holster and his eyes on the sumptuous Angela Larkin, Gunn goes off hot—on his enemy's trail!

GUNN #4: BLOOD JUSTICE (670, $1.95)
Gunn is enticed into playing a round with a ruthless gambling scoundrel. He also plays a round with the scoundrel's estranged wife—and the stakes are on the rise!

GUNN #5: WINTER HELL (708, $1.95)
Gunn's journey west arouses more than his suspicion and fear. Especially when he comes across the remains of an Indian massacre—and winds up with a ripe young beauty on his hands . . .

GUNN #6: DUEL IN PERGATORY (739, $1.95)
Someone in Oxley's gang is out to get Gunn. That's the only explanation for the sniper on his trail. But Oxley's wife is out to get him too—in a very different way.

GUNN #7: LAW OF THE ROPE (766, $1.95)
The sheriff's posse wants to string Gunn up on the spot—for a murder he didn't commit. And the only person who can save him is the one who pointed the finger at him from the start: the victim's young and luscious daughter!

Available wherever paperbacks are sold, or order direct from the Publisher. Send cover price plus 50¢ per copy for mailing and handling to Zebra Books, 475 Park Avenue South, New York, N.Y. 10016. DO NOT SEND CASH.

DON'T MISS THESE HEROIC FANTASY FAVORITES
BY MIKE SIROTA

RO-LAN #1: MASTER OF BORANGA (616, $1.95)
Swept into a strange, other dimensional world, Ro-lan is forced to fight for his life and the woman he loves against man, beast, and the all-powerful evil dictator, the MASTER OF BORANGA.

RO-LAN #2: THE SHROUDED WALLS OF BORANGA (677, $1.95)
Love and loyalty drive fearless and dashing Ro-lan to return to the horrifying isle of Boranga. But even if he succeeds in finding and crossing through the warp again, could he hope to escape that evil place of strange and hostile creatures?

RO-LAN #3: JOURNEY TO MESHARRA (726, $2.25)
Pitted against a savage horde of Amazons, terrible sea creatures and a horrid bloodletting ceremony, Ro-lan and his faithful companions undertake a journey into the dominion of an ancient Mesharran—whose legendary powers may equal those of the Master of Boranga!

THE TWENTIETH SON OF ORNON (685, $1.95)
Dulok, the twentieth son of Ornon, is determined to become the Survivor—the sole ruler of the mighty kingdom of Shadzea. But he is also determined to avenge the death of his mother—whose blood was spilled by the great Ornon himself!

Available wherever paperbacks are sold, or order direct from the Publisher. Send cover price plus 50¢ per copy for mailing and handling to Zebra Books, 475 Park Avenue South, New York, N.Y. 10016. DO NOT SEND CASH.

READ THESE HORRIFYING BEST SELLERS!

THE WITCHING (746, $2.75)
by Fritzen Ravenswood
A spine-tingling story of witchcraft and Satanism unfolds as a powerful coven seeks unrelenting revenge!

MOONDEATH (702, $2.75)
by Rick Hautala
A peaceful New England town is stalked by a blood-thirsty werewolf. *"One of the best horror novels I've ever read..."*—Stephen King

THE DEVIL'S KISS (717, $2.75)
by William W. Johnstone
The Devil has waited for hundreds of years to take over the prairie town of Whitfield. The time has finally come—will anyone be able to stop his powers of evil once they've been unleashed...?

CHERRON (700, $2.50)
by Sharon Combes
A young girl, taunted and teased for her physical imperfections, uses her telekinetic powers to wreak bloody vengeance on her tormentors—body and soul!

THE NEST (662, $2.50)
by Gregory A. Douglas
An ordinary garbage dump in a small quiet town becomes the site of incredible horror when a change in poison control causes huge mutant creatures to leave their nest in search of human flesh.

Available wherever paperbacks are sold, or order direct from the Publisher. Send cover price plus 50¢ per copy for mailing and handling to Zebra Books, 475 Park Avenue South, New York, N.Y. 10016. DO NOT SEND CASH.

TROUBLE-SHOOTING WESTERNS

AMBUSH RANGE (696, $1.95)
by Don P. Jenison
When Buck Randall returns to Bear Valley for his Brother's funeral, he stumbles into a cache of rustled cattle and a violent feud between families. But will he stumble across the man who shot his brother—or will he have to search him out?

THE BRONCBUSTER (671, $1.95)
by Mick Clumpner
Ross Dunbar is a broncbuster out of work, but when he wanders onto A K Ranch he finds plenty of it—dodging four armed men looking for a stranger to pin a murder rap on!

HARD TRAIL TO SANTA FE (676, $1.95)
by Tom West
Glory, gold and adventure attracted hundreds to the new trading route opening to Santa Fe. But Red Blake joined for a darker reason: Somewhere in the great Taos slave market, he hoped to find his wife. . . .

BLOOD ON THE RANGE (686, $1.95)
by Owen G. Irons
After spending eighteen years in prison for a murder he didn't commit, Ford finally returned to his home town. With his true love lost and his father dead, he swelled with smoldering resentment and cried bloody revenge!

GALLOWS GOLD (687, $1.95)
by James Parrette
Money is always at the root of Charlie Morgan's mistakes—especially when he shoots a man in the back to get it and finds that the price the law puts on his head is not what he'd bargained for!

Available wherever paperbacks are sold, or order direct from the Publisher. Send cover price plus 50¢ per copy for mailing and handling to Zebra Books, 475 Park Avenue South, New York, N.Y. 10016. DO NOT SEND CASH.